The Summer Meadows

The Summer Meadows

ROBERT NATHAN

74-781

DELACORTE PRESS / NEW YORK

Library of Congress Cataloging in Publication Data

Nathan, Robert, 1894–
  The summer meadows.
  I. Title
PZ3.N195Sw [PS3527.A74]   813'.5'4   73–5829

There were three of us: Larry, Herbie, and I.
And then there was Ruth,
and that made four.

Old friend, we have come into the shadowy part of the woods,
The gray seventies. The path is rougher, and grows narrower,
The legs tremble a little, the breath is shorter.
We look anxiously about. Creatures of bad intent are here;
The path could end suddenly.

                            Behind, in summer meadows,
The live, bright figures come and go. They are far away,
Smaller and smaller, seen for a moment and lost again,
Golden, tiny creatures, in and out of the sun, ourselves

                                    among them,
Leaping and darting, dancing in butterfly clusters,
Singing of love, singing of youth eternal.

                          It was all there once.
It is all there still.

                          We go forward into the forest.
We can never go back to join them. We can never return there.

On starting a Journey, it is of the utmost importance to take a loving thought along.

A TRAVELLER'S GUIDE,
by the Reverend Alexander Winnifrith
(Cordelia's great-great-grandfather),
London, 1810.

The Summer Meadows

Chapter 1

WE had been walking in the rose garden, my wife
Cordelia and I. It is her garden really, because she is an
Englishwoman who talks to flowers. They bloom under
her care and never talk back, which makes it possible for
her to express those opinions which I have begged her to
hide from our friends. For she is a Victorian at heart
and believes in authority, goodness, and Genesis 1 and 2.

And like so many Victorians, she believes in love,
which is a great comfort to me, because it is generally
held in contempt these days. I believe in it too. But
about Genesis, I am with Dr. Leakey.

For some reason, our conversation had touched upon
the good doctor's work in Africa. Cordelia lifted her

chin in the way she had, a gesture at once enchanting
and formidable.

"I will never believe," she declared, "that I am
descended from some apelike creature. God made man in
His own image, and we have His word for it."

As a clergyman's daughter, she had been brought up
on the Bible. "I am not a monkey's daughter," she
announced firmly. "My ancestor was Adam."

"I know," I said, for I never disagreed with her about
anything on which she had set her heart. My private
thoughts about space and time, the mysterious universe,
and God's curious choice of Abraham as a confidant, I
preferred to keep to myself. "His wife was Eve, and they
had two sons, Cain and Abel. And when Cain slew Abel,
he went toward the east, to the Land of Nod, and
married."

"Yes," she agreed. "So he did."

"Whom did he marry?" I asked.

"I'm sure I don't know," said Cordelia. "Nor do I
care."

"Isn't it odd," I said, "that there should have been
other people in the world besides Adam and Eve?"

She wrinkled up her nose, thinking about it. "Well,
there could have been," she said at last. "There might
have been daughters."

"Besides, people lived a lot longer in those days; look

at Methusaleh. Adam could have had a lot of children and grandchildren—even great-great-grandchildren."

And she concluded comfortably:

"Anyway, it all happened in Mesopotamia."

"Cordelia," I said, "I love you. No one else would countenance a man marrying his own great-great-great-niece simply because he wasn't an Englishman. However, the truth is, the Land of Nod was a land of sorcerers. Cain's wife was not a woman at all, she was a witch. That is why today almost all women are half Eve's daughter and half witch."

"Thank you, darling," said Cordelia. "I love you too." And pointing to one of the roses, she exclaimed:

"Look how well my Countess Vandal is coming along. Dear Lady Vandal, you have aphids."

Under the broad-brimmed hat she wore, to keep her skin from browning in the hot California sun, my wife who, at fifty, still had her English complexion—that of a lily crossed ever so lightly with a rose—turned troubled blue eyes on me. "Robbie," she asked, "do you think that flowers cry out sometimes when they are hurt?"

"It's possible," I said. "They may even utter the primal scream which is so popular today. Perhaps in the future we may have a way of recording it, but as of now, it's all part of the mystery. Because, my darling, Bible or no Bible . . ."

"I know," she said, "you're going to tell me about all the things we don't know."

And she bent down to pluck a snail from the stalk of a tuberose begonia. "It's unsettling," she said.

I replied that we were living in unsettled times. "Every now and then, the world goes through such a period. Imagine with what anxiety people must have lived through the fall of Rome."

"I should rather think they might have done," she agreed.

I sighed. "One is so close to death these days," I began and then broke off, not knowing how to go on. Because, in fact, I had been thinking about death a great deal; one does, as one approaches seventy.

"It makes me very angry when you talk that way," said Cordelia. She spoke firmly and with absolute conviction. She was convinced that we would live to be a hundred. After that . . .

But that, of course, was what tantalized me. To Cordelia, it was as simple as that Victorian England in which she felt at home: she would be reunited somewhere, somehow, with all the good and dear people of the past, including her parents, her nanny, and Lord Nelson, who was her one secret and abiding love. (She did not, of course, expect to find Emma at his side.) To me, on the other hand, it was—like God—incomprehensible. In my happier moments, I saw it as a kind of soundless light, into which one would go, with whatever love one had at hand.

When we returned to the house, the morning mail had already been delivered, and Cordelia sat down at once to glance through the advertisements in *Country Life*, a magazine which arrived every month from London. For although she had lived the past thirty years in America, my wife was still homesick for England and still hoped, after all those years, and at my age, to wheedle me into exchanging our small, comfortable California house, set on a hill above the sea, for the meadowy summers and dreadful winters of Kent or Devonshire.

"Darling," she explained, "there's a heavenly cottage in Hampshire right on the River Ichen, for only eighteen thousand pounds."

"It has only one bathroom," I said idly, riffling through my mail. There was a letter from my old school friend Larry—to be opened last, an exhortation from the Salvation Army, three bills (one overdue), and a catalog from a mail-order company.

"How did you know?" she demanded.

"Because," I explained, "each bathroom in an English house is valued at ten thousand pounds. So the same

cottage with two bathrooms would be priced at twenty-
eight thousand. I've made a study of it."

"Oh—you Americans and your bathrooms!"

"My dear," I said, "you lived in a sixteenth-century
mansion with thirty rooms and one bathroom upstairs
under the eaves. There was a loo on the ground floor, and
you used chamber pots."

"A loo is much better outside the bathroom than in
it," she countered. "And anyway, it wasn't a mansion, but
a rectory with eight rooms. We did live in a mansion
later, when father died, and the bishop let us live in a
wing of Restoration House with a marvelous ghost. . . .
Darling, what is it?"

For I had opened Larry's letter, and my dismay was
all too evident. "He says that Herbie's dying," I said
stupidly.

"Oh dear!" she whispered and looked at me, her eyes
brimming with sympathy and sorrow.

There had always been the three of us—Larry, Herbie,
and myself—ever since I could remember. Life had
separated us, given us different roles to play: Larry the
physician, Herbie the professor, and I the novelist; but
the tie, almost like a family tie that bound us together,
had never come undone.

"Well," I said after a while, "I suppose we knew it
was coming." For Herbie had been ill for more than a

year, watched over—sometimes from a distance—by Larry, nursed and comforted by Herbie's wife, Ruth. Or, perhaps—and that was what was so sad about it—not always comforted.

Because Herbie was not easily comforted by anyone, nor had been for a long, long time.

Chapter 2

THE gray evening fog came in off the sea as usual, damp and cold—except that it seemed colder than usual. Or perhaps I only thought so. Herbie dying . . . ? I had been right to think about death; my whole generation was dying, disappearing into history where its heroes would be reconsidered by those who never knew them, its values pondered and judged—the true heroes forgotten in favor of others better publicized or with louder friends, its values laughed at or misunderstood.

And Herbie—and I—would we be understood? I doubted it. It didn't seem to matter; what mattered was the moment of dying, that mysterious moment. . . .

For a while, earlier, I had toyed with the idea of flying

east to be with him. But then I thought, no, Ruth would be with him, and that was the only really important thing. Ruth had always been with him.

I lit a fire against the fog and sat by it and listened to the logs crackling and the faint fall of the surf from the ocean below. The tide was going out; I knew the whispering sound of it. Cordelia had gone upstairs to bed. "Don't think too much about it, my darling," she had said. "Herbie is in God's hands now."

I smiled at her and pressed the palm of her hand, soft as a rose petal, against my cheek. God's hands, I thought wryly; He has no hands, but I didn't say it. It didn't seem the right moment for theological discussions.

We had been so young together once, the three of us—Herbie, Larry, and I. And what great hopes we'd had . . . hopes of the world—the new world that was to be free and friendly, full of order, beauty, and truth. And in which Herbie would be, most of all, a moving spirit, because of his position in the government, his Pulitzer Prize, his extraordinary mind. . . . It was the mind of an Edwardian, with its strange courtliness: questioning, impatient, expressing itself in grave harmonies of prose and sudden, boisterous, almost childlike humor. Loving—and cantankerous

There had seemed to be no end to what we would accomplish, once we had set our minds to it. And what

had we accomplished? Nothing. The great wars had
swept us aside like kindling. For all our hopes, for all
our efforts, the future had left us behind.

I thought about the past, and how we had traveled
here and there, sometimes together, but mostly apart. It
seemed to me that we were always going somewhere, in
search of—what? Long journeys . . . some no more than
a mile or two in length, but a thousand miles in the spirit.
I remember walking home to our rooms at Harvard from
a performance of the Boston Symphony. It was an evening
in winter, and the air, already blue with dusk, was cold as
ice water. Herbie was without a hat; his dark, curly hair
framed his face which was glowing and joyous. We had
been on a long voyage from César Franck to Brahms; in
the clear, pale, wintry sky, the evening star hung above
Cambridge like Franck's pure and lonely flute.

"The old ones," said Herbie, "have laid down a path
for us; we need only to follow it. Onward and upward.
It's a beautiful world, Bobby, and we should all be as
happy as kings.

"Providing," he added sensibly, "that we get through
our midyear exams."

There was no problem of that kind for Herbie, for he
graduated with high honors.

The war to end all wars came, and he joined the navy,

winning a commission finally as a lieutenant j.g.—for which I promptly, and ever after, named him Admiral. He taught me a quarterdeck exercise: a dozen steps forward, a step back, a smart turn, and a dozen steps in the opposite direction. The war taught me nothing else— not even to doubt the path laid down.

I, too, made voyages, to the south and to the west and back again to New York, to the Village, where I had a little studio room on West Ninth Street. And there Herbie, back from one of his own journeys—this one to Kansas, where he had gone to take up a teaching job at the university—first met Ruth, tall, freckled, blonde, lately graduated from Vassar, and presently working in the offices of *The Dial*, and immediately fell in love with her, as she with him, where he sat huddled, dark, romantic, aloof, underneath my piano. "I shall be safe there," he had said, disliking crowds and shy of strangers, but he was mistaken. "Bobby," Ruth declared later that evening, "I have never seen anyone so beautiful in my life." They were married a year later and moved to Lawrence, Kansas, where he was installed as an assistant professor of economics at the university.

I remember a visit to them, to the old, wooden, verandahed house in which they lived; how we drove through the Kansas countryside, talking of happiness;

and how valorously Herbie handled his first small automobile; and how he shouted with exuberance at the way Ruth had cooked a ham—a whole half a ham which, by the way, we continued to eat in one form or another during the entire four days of my visit. "There are pineapples in it!" he cried, as though he had just been made a Christmas gift of unbelievable magnificence, and ever after, if there was something good to be said about anything, it "had pineapples in it."

And, later by only a few years, the house in Geneva, Switzerland, where Herbie and Ruth lived while Herbie worked for the International Labor Organization at the League of Nations; and how the sun shone down on us, on Ruth's wheat-colored hair, and the warmth of her love—for him, of course, but for all of us really—myself, Larry and Larry's wife, and visiting friends . . . and how, now that his voice was beginning to be heard in the world of economics and political science, Herbie would flash suddenly into anger at some obstinate or complacent colleague. I remembered the long evening before the fire, Ruth and Herbie hand in hand, while the victrola played records from the operas; or lunches in the sunny garden; or at dusk in the shadows on the verandah—the five of us, Larry and his wife, Herbie, Ruth, myself . . . what laughter, what bright hopes! A glowing memory. We would all be great some day, and the world would be made safe forever. We would all have a hand in it, but Herbie most of all. And we were all of us young, and none of us would ever grow old. There really were pineapples in it.

As I sat there, before the fire, I thought back to the twenties, the golden years of my generation. There seemed no end to delight; a whole generation of young men and women poured out upon the world like children on a holiday, exploding into joy, into poetry, into cries of passion, into liberty, dying of alcohol, dancing in fountains. In Paris, the young writers gathered at the Dome or the Rotonde, made love under the loom of Sacre Coeur, or along the shadowy quays. In the spring the chestnut trees blossomed, in winter the odor of roasting chestnuts warmed the rain-driven streets. There the legends were born, the heroes announced—those who, like Hemingway and Fitzgerald, would die following their own legends to the end.

And love . . . love was like the sunlight on the chestnut trees, like the light clouds that floated in the south above the Auvergne. With whom wasn't I in love?

> By brooks too broad for leaping
>   The light-foot boys are laid;
> The rose-lipt girls are sleeping
>   In fields where roses fade.

Marriage: that was something of a different sort. No
river in spate, breathtaking, brawling, but a sea on which
one could voyage endlessly under the brightest sky,
untroubled and serene.

And so, it seemed, was Herbie's marriage in those
days. His quarrels at the Labor Office with Arthur Sweetser
disturbed but failed to threaten his exuberance. The
snowy shoulders of Mont Blanc in the pure air above
us, the shining lake, the speeches, the sense of important
things stirring . . . breakfasts of chocolate, croissants, and
honey in the bee-loud, wasp-lashed garden . . . Ruth busy
in her kitchen experimenting with sauces . . . and all of
us on our way, upward and onward . . . to what?

To the Depression, to the end of an era. To the
years which turned the world forever away from the old,
comforting certainties and set it on the path to heaven
knows what.

Curiously, the Depression led the three of us upward
rather than downward. Larry set out his shingle as a
psychoanalyst, I wrote my first successful novel, and
Herbie was called to Washington by President Hoover
to give advice to the State Department. By that time his
hair, once so dark and curly, had turned white. He was
much too young for such a thing to have happened—but
there it was—almost snowy, in fact. It gave him a look
half elder-statesman, half pixie: Cicero and Puck

combined. Ruth loved it. He used to worry one lock of it when deep in thought.

When did things begin to go wrong for them? I don't know. They had a charming house in Georgetown, and there Ruth entertained members of foreign delegations as well as officials of the various departments of our own government. She delighted in protocol. "You see," she said solemnly, "it's very important to know exactly who you are. For instance: we go into dinner before the assistant secretaries, because Herbie is head of his own department. We *follow* the Under-Secretary, of course, and the Speaker and people like that—the Supreme Court Justices and all, and the ambassadors. At least, I think we do; I'll have to find out. We're about half way down the list, between the President and the bottom; that's where the representatives are, on the bottom, unless they're the chairman of the ways and means committee—

"Oh Bobby," she cried, clapping her hands, "isn't it fun?"

But a moment later, she turned serious. "Herbie hates it," she said.

I didn't think he hated it really. But he had little patience with politicking, the constant conniving for position; he resented the struggle for influence. It was not for nothing that I called him "Admiral"; there was something bluff and salty about him.

"Herbie," said Ruth solemnly, "is absolutely undeviating. And, of course, always right." She was loyalty itself.

But there was still a great deal of laughter, even in Washington. The days were an excitement, an adventure. "Don't be surprised," he told Ruth on their way to the White House, "if the President calls me Herbie. That's his way; he likes that."

"I know, dear," said Ruth. "And we call him Mr. President. He likes that too."

"Don't be idiotic," said Herbie.

During the Depression I visited the house in Georgetown for the first time. A slim, cool, white house, with formal though not very large rooms, it was a far cry from the old, wooden, verandahed house in Lawrence, Kansas. In it, Herbie and Ruth gave small, formal dinners, entertained foreign trade commissions, bureau chiefs, occasional legislators, and officials of the administration. They had few friends in Washington outside of government, and Herbert chafed at the need to keep his opinions to himself, to be wary, and to be correct. Yet, when he was with one of his old friends—an outsider, so to speak—he felt constrained; there were so many things he couldn't talk about—so many state secrets, so many private memoranda from government, so much information not for public ears. "Damn it,

Bobby!" he exclaimed, exasperated. "I could tell you things. Only, I can't."

So many journeys for them, then and later: north, south, east, and west; to England, France, Spain, the Orient; journeys for the State Department and later for himself, voyages in search of letters, documents, in libraries, government archives, private homes—the historian's quest. Begun so long ago, in Boston, in Kansas, in Geneva . . .

And now, in his great house in Maine, above the swift, green, tidal river, he had come to the end of voyaging. He lay there in his bed . . . I could imagine it. Aware, impatient, irascible, impatient to be away. For the last time. And on a voyage from which he would never bring back any history at all.

In the quiet of my room, in the lamp and firelight, the remembered sound of that tidal river merged with the soft hiss and plop of the logs in my fireplace and the whisper of the surf below my windows. Lost in memories, I had fallen into a state of semisomnolence, when I heard—or thought I heard—the front door open and close. It took a moment or two for me to register it in my mind, during which I thought—vaguely and foolishly —that it might have been Cordelia. Foolishly, because she was in bed upstairs. But even so, I was not alarmed.

"Who is it?" I asked, rousing myself only a little.

The figure that came into the room was familiar, yet strange; for it had no business to be there at all.

"Bobby?" it said half questioningly.

I sat bolt upright, startled and shocked.

"*Herbie?*"

It couldn't be, but it was. He looked thinner and younger than the last time I'd seen him, and some of his old assurance seemed to have been drained out of him. He glanced uncertainly around the room and then looked at me almost guiltily.

"Bobby," he said—and I realized that it was in the voice of his younger days—

"I'm lost."

Chapter 3

WE sat and stared at each other helplessly. Lost? What did he mean? How could he be lost?—since there he was, sitting across from me. Yet, at the same time—how could he be there at all? He was dying . . . three thousand miles away—

"Herbie," I said half joyfully, half fearfully, "this isn't possible." *74-781*

"It isn't exactly where I set out for," he admitted guiltily.

"But I thought—" I exclaimed, "—at least, Larry wrote . . ."

He nodded calmly. "Oh, that's all over," he declared.

I felt a rush of relief. "Thank heavens," I said. "I was afraid . . ."

"Nothing to be afraid of any more, Bobby," he said.

He was silent for a moment, pulling at a lock of his hair in the way I remembered. "Though I confess," he said presently, "I was a little afraid too, for a while."

He looked around the room again and shook his head. "There are still a few things I don't remember," he said, "but it's a comfort to be here."

"It's wonderful to see you," I said. But something in his expression, or in his manner, troubled me. "Are you sure you're all right?" I asked. "Because—"

He gazed at me gravely. "I was going on a journey, Bobby," he declared, "a journey of some importance. A final and most hopeful attempt to find certain source material for my history. I had a destination, but for some reason Ruth failed to make the usual travel arrangements."

"How is she?" I asked. It was a banal question, but I tried to make it sound eager. The shadow of a frown crossed his face. "She's getting old," he said, "and forgetful. But she's all right."

He was silent again. "I left her in good company," he said slowly, at last. "A lot of our friends were there. Old friends and some relatives. She seemed composed."

"Tell me," he said after a moment, "how is Cordelia?"

"She's fine," I said. "A little tired from working in her rose garden. She went to bed."

He seemed relieved. "Good," he said. "I'm glad all's well with you both. The arbutus was just coming out at home."

"You should have let us know you were coming," I told him. "We'd have had a room ready for you."

He smiled gently and, I thought, a little sadly. "No need, Bobby," he said. "Don't trouble yourself. Besides— how could I have let you know? When I didn't know myself?"

"It's no trouble, actually," I said. "Cordelia can make up a bed in the spare room . . ."

He shook his head. "I don't want a bed," he said. "I'm tired to death of beds. What with the damn doctors poking at me every other minute . . ."

He gave me one of his eager, youthful smiles. "Let's just sit and talk, shall we?"

"All night?"

"It wouldn't be the first time, Bobby."

No, I thought, it wouldn't be the first time. And I thought of the time we'd ridden up and down Fifth Avenue all night on top of a bus—the tops of Fifth Avenue buses were open in those days—and then sat on the curb at Fifty-ninth Street, with our feet in the gutter, watching the dawn come up, watching the night clouds rolling away over the Hudson, the high windows of the great apartment buildings across the park flaming

into gold as the first rays of the sun hit them, the dawn
sky in the north brightening, the rosy orange morning
rising behind us, the floodlight of clear blue day flowing
over everything, over the city and the great buildings,
yellow and white in the sun. What had we talked
about then? I didn't remember.

There were no open bus tops any more, and no sun
was coming up. "The trouble was," said Herbie, "there
were always too many people to please."

I knew that he was thinking of his days as economic
advisor. Caught between a weak though amiable
Secretary of State and a brilliant but incalculable
President, he had suffered endless frustration. And at
each new blow—to his plans, his ideals, his pride—he
had aimed his anger at the only target he had—his wife.
I remembered sitting in the prim living room of the
Georgetown house and hearing him raging and bellowing
upstairs.

As I remembered her, she was always—as he had
described her—composed. But that afternoon she came
downstairs with a stricken look.

"It was that damned Harry White," he said suddenly,
as though he too had been remembering those days. "And
Morgenthau. I had to battle every day for State against
the Treasury. And I lost every battle."

Poor Herbie—at once so high and so lowly; caught

in the vortex, in the opposing currents; his voice muted by
political considerations. I knew that he blamed himself
for not having done more and, blaming himself, turned
his anger and frustration on Ruth—for the same reason
that men climb mountains; because she was there. One
does that in families; I had done it myself, both as a child
and, later, as a husband. But my own failures were
private and modest; I was never so near the seat of power
or so helpless to influence it.

I remembered, too, another look on Ruth's face, a
look of such pity and at the same time embarrassment,
as though she were hurt both for him and for herself.
The occasion was a Sunday luncheon at the house of two
dear friends—a beautiful home in Rye, looking out over
the Sound, the gardens, the green fields sloping to the
shore, and Long Island blue and misty across the water.
A naval captain was there, just returned from convoy
duty; the year was 1940, and we were not yet at war, but
our cruisers were escorting our merchant ships across the
Atlantic to and from Britain. Grim and tense, he told us
how he had seen one of his tankers torpedoed by German
submarines almost under his nose and how he had watched
men drowning in the sea alight with burning fuel. "Those
subs," he exclaimed in an agitated voice, "had refueled
in Spanish ports. By God, if I could get my hands on
whoever was responsible for sending that oil to Spain . . ."

23

Herbie got up from the table, excused himself as having a pressing engagement in town, and left without a further word. He did not return that day.

"Why, Herbie?" I asked him now.

He sighed. "It was the decision of the Iberian Peninsular Committee," he said slowly, "to keep sending a certain amount of oil to Spain, for fear that if we did not, Franco would turn finally to the Axis, strike at Gibraltar, and close the Strait. Whether we were right or wrong . . . I don't know. No one knew about the committee; it was secret.

"And I was its chairman."

"It was all long ago," I said.

"Not to a historian."

"Most people have forgotten. To the young today, Hitler and his Nazis never existed. They're figures in a wax museum. Like Attila. Like Queen Victoria."

"Not to me. I had to deal with them."

"You left Ruth in a state that day," I said.

He was silent for a moment. "There were times," he said at last, "when I was scarcely aware of her."

"And other times," I reminded him, "when you cursed her."

He nodded soberly. "And yet," I persisted, "you never left her."

"How could I have left her?" he demanded. "She was a part of me."

He stretched out his hands in an appealing gesture. "What is it about marriage, Bobby?" he asked. "Sometimes I hated her."

"As you say, she was a part of you."

He shook his head despondently. "The world went down, and I went down with it."

"You went down with it," I told him. "But she didn't."

His voice grew sharp. "She's a fool, Bobby," he said. "An old, obstinate fool."

"Of course," I agreed. "If she hadn't been, she'd never have stayed with you."

"Why did she, then?"

"Why? Because she loved you. You were her world. Even your white hair . . . She thought you were beautiful."

He looked at me sadly. "But difficult?" he asked.

I nodded. "Yes, indeed," I said. "As long as we're being honest."

I looked at him curiously. He seemed more uncertain and disturbed than I ever remembered to have seen him—except, perhaps, during those days just before the war, when he was struggling with the problems of anti-

Semitism, isolationism, pro-Teutonism, and politics as usual. But he was angry then. Now he looked sad and lonely.

"Would you like to phone her?" I asked. He shook his head. "It's too late," he said. "She wouldn't answer."

He was right, of course; it would have been almost two in the morning at York, and Ruth would have been asleep.

"Look," I said, "there's no help for it. Whether you like it or not, you'll have to stay the night. I'll tell Cordelia. . . ."

"No," he said sharply. "Please." And he added more gently, "I don't want to disturb her."

"Well, then," I said, "I'll find a bed for you myself."

He seemed to retreat into himself, to become, somehow, smaller and helpless. "Very well," he said in a curiously resigned voice. "I suppose there's no help for it. Any bed will do, Bobby. Let's not make any trouble."

He sagged back in his chair and closed his eyes. "I am tired," he confessed. "And confused. Perhaps in the morning . . ."

His voice trailed away into silence, he was asleep. I covered him with the afghan from the couch and left him and went upstairs. Cordelia was sleeping on her side, as always, one hand beneath her cheek, the other curled peacefully beside her. "Darling," I whispered, "we have company."

She didn't wake, but she stirred and sighed, her lips opened slightly, and I thought she said something. I bent over her, the better to hear.

"I know," she whispered. "Herbie's here."

Chapter 4

I WOKE in the bright morning to find Cordelia leaning on one elbow, looking at me in a puzzled way. "Robbie," she said, "did I dream it? Or did we actually have a visitor last night?"

It took me a moment to gather myself together. "Yes," I said. "I thought you . . ."

"It was Herbie, wasn't it?" she asked, frowning, as though she were trying to believe something she didn't believe.

I nodded. "Is he still here?" she asked, wondering.

"Yes," I said. "At least—I suppose so. Unless . . ."

"Why didn't you tell me?"

"But I did," I said. "And anyway—he didn't want to disturb you."

She sat up abruptly. "Darling," she said, "we'd best get downstairs."

She threw on a bathrobe, and I followed her, stumbling a little in my still half-awake state. But the living room was empty.

We stood looking at each other helplessly. "I left him asleep in the chair," I said. "Right there. I covered him over. . . ."

I had never seen Cordelia so troubled. "Robbie," she said, "this is altogether too strange. Are you quite sure? I have the queerest feeling. . . ."

"He said he was on his way to somewhere or other. . . ."

"He didn't say where?"

"No," I declared. "He said he was lost."

"Lost? But darling . . . *lost?* How very odd?"

"It was odd," I admitted, "the whole thing was odd. I don't know . . . I've no idea where he could have gone."

"And you're sure he was here?"

"He was here," I said. "In that chair. I didn't dream it, if that's what you mean."

"If you dreamt it," she said slowly, "I dreamt it too."

"Well," I said, "we'll have to wait and see."

But at that moment, Herbie himself appeared in the doorway leading to the garden. Framed in the sunlight, he looked younger than he had; apparently the night's sleep, however uncomfortable, had refreshed him.

"Good morning," he said. "I've been enjoying your garden, Cordelia."

I saw the color rush to Cordelia's face. "Herbie!" she cried, going toward him with arms outstretched. "Why didn't you let Robbie wake me? You must have been cold and famished. . . . He probably didn't even offer you a cup of tea! What would you like for breakfast? I'll have some coffee on in a moment. . . ."

"Dear Cordelia," he said smiling. "I've already had my breakfast. But I'll sit with you while you have yours, if I may."

His dark eyes smiled with affection at us both. "All your roses, Cordelia," he said. "What a splendid show! The Garden at York is in full flower too. June was white with lilies-of-the-valley; they looked like little snowfields under the great oaks and beeches, above the green flowing river. . . ." His voice trailed off, and his face took on a dreamy look. "It's good to be here with you," he said. "But I can't stay very long."

"I hope," said Cordelia, "that at least . . ."

"You see," he went on earnestly, but at the same time a little puzzled, "you see, I'm really on a journey, one of those endless journeys a historian undertakes to unearth someone's private papers, hidden away in some library or someone's attic. . . ."

He hesitated a moment. "A memory," he said. "I'm not sure of what I shall find, but I know that it is of the utmost importance.

"I was quite clear when I started out. But Ruth . . ."

He made an irritated gesture with both hands. "Bobby probably told you," he said to Cordelia. "Ruth forgot to make the arrangements."

"We'll try to reach her," said Cordelia soothingly. "We'll get everything straightened out. Meanwhile I'm going to make up the spare room for you. You must rest; you could do with a nap. After the night you must have had."

"Actually," said Herbie, "it was a strangely luminous night. I've known nights like it in York, when the fog seemed to collect star-shine and to glow with a light of its own. And the same stillness. And under the stillness the sound of the river like the sound of time draining out to sea."

"You heard the sea itself," I said. "It's just down the hill a ways, behind us."

"Come along," Cordelia told him. "I'm putting you to bed."

"Very well," he said, "if you must, you must." And turning to me, he added with a smile whose sudden sparkle reminded me of long ago:

"What a domineering woman! Why do you put up

with it?" With which he followed Cordelia meekly though a trifle laboriously up the stairs, and I went to the telephone to ring Ruth in New England.

It was a while before I reached the house at York, for the circuits to Maine were busy. And when I finally reached the house, there was no reply at first, and then a strange voice answered. Ruth was not taking any calls; "if I would please leave my name . . ."

"That's odd," I said to Cordelia when she joined me downstairs again. "Ruthie isn't taking any calls."

"What's odd about it?" she asked. "She's probably exhausted, the poor darling. Tired out. Because if Herbie is really . . ."

Her eyes widened, she clapped her hand to her mouth, and we stared at each other in bewilderment. "Wait a minute," I said. "Wait a minute."

"Darling," she said, "there's something awfully fishy here."

"I know," I agreed. "And I don't understand it. Unless I misread Larry's letter. Could he have said 'flying'?"

She shook her head. "He definitely said 'dying.' "

"Well," I said helplessly, "he was wrong, apparently."

"He must have been, mustn't he."

"Of course," I reasoned, "Herbie has been ill for a long time. Ruthie has been under a terrific strain."

"She's upset," said Cordelia firmly. "So should I be. She doesn't want to talk to anyone. She didn't want him to go on this trip—whatever it is. And he probably shouldn't have gone."

"By the way," she asked, looking around, "where are his bags?"

"He didn't have any," I said.

We were both silent, looking at each other. "Darling," she said at last, "it really does seem a bit odd. Do you think we ought to try to get through to Larry?"

"Yes," I said. "I do."

But no one answered the phone at Larry's apartment in Baltimore, and from his answering service in Towson I merely learned that he was out of town. "Well," I said, "there's nothing we can do for a while, anyway. Not until after his nap."

"I'm going out into the garden," said Cordelia, "and talk to my roses."

And as she left the room, she added firmly:

"Not to worry."

It was always a comfort to have her tell me with such assurance not to worry. It is characteristic of the English to look at things optimistically, with confidence that somehow or other everything will turn out all right in the end. I have often wondered where it came from, this confidence: from the Celts? the Romans? It is not a virtue to be found in any one of them singly—nor in the Phoenicians toiling up the windy blue-green valleys of the Atlantic on their way to Cornwall for tin.

Still, it was odd. I knew that Ruth had always packed Herbie's bags for him—a fact that often enough in the past had brought about an outburst of irritation from him, when, as occasionally, he found himself minus some crucial bit of clothing, a dress tie, a set of braces, a pair of cuff links. Only, this time, she had apparently forgotten to pack at all. She hadn't sent him off as she had always done, she hadn't made the usual traveling arrangements for him, and she wouldn't answer the phone.

They must have disagreed very bitterly about something, I thought.

It was a bright California day, and the sea below our hill shone blue and peaceful in the sun. I could hear the usual traffic on the coast road in front of the house, and I was turning back from the open doorway when I was attracted by a most unusual sound—the clop, clop of a horse's hooves on the cement highway, and looking around, I was surprised to see a van driven by an elderly figure turn in at our driveway and draw up in front of the house. A horse-drawn cart was unusual enough, but the shape of it struck me as even stranger, for it appeared to be a sort of gipsy caravan, built on the remains of an old-fashioned hearse. Brightly painted and drawn by a meek and ancient horse, it bore the sign, MORTIMER'S ANTIQUES AND CURIO SHOP, along its side.

The driver climbed down from his perch and approached me hat in hand. He was, as I have said, elderly; at least he gave the impression of being old, but how old I had no idea. His face was unlined, but ordinary in the extreme; his expression polite but dogged. He could have been a bailiff or a civil servant of some sort on an errand for the court or for the city.

"I have come," he said, "to inquire if you have any antiques which you might be willing to let me have."

I looked around for Cordelia, but she was in the rose garden toward the rear of the house and out of sight. "Well, now," I began, "I scarcely think . . ."

He held up his hand in an oddly quieting way. "I am in the market for everything and anything," he said. "Old things, used things . . ."

"Why no," I said. "I don't think we have anything of that kind."

He looked at me quietly, without expression. I could see that he didn't believe me, but he didn't try to push or to argue with me. "Perhaps later," he said. And he added simply:

"I shall be around for a bit."

So saying, he climbed back onto his van and, with a courteous nod of his head, drove slowly away.

"Really," said Cordelia, when I told her about it later, "it has been a very strange day on the whole. I think I'll make myself a nice cup of tea."

Herbie slept until evening. At dinner he seemed relaxed; there were moments when the Herbie I used to know rippled to the surface as he poked gentle fun at Cordelia or myself or told us some story of long ago, when he traveled with the Secretary of War through the Islands to Japan. At other times he seemed to withdraw, to be far away in his thoughts, as though pondering on his present journey. I knew that he must be anxious, and Cordelia knew it too and did her best to reassure him. "I'm sure it will all be straightened out in the morning," she declared, but I knew that her confidence was assumed, that she was really worried and had Ruth on her mind.

Toward the end of dinner, Herbie seemed to brighten up to the point of asking me how my own work was going. "Not very well," I told him and caught a quick look of distress on Cordelia's face. "The fact is," she explained, "that Robbie thinks he's out of tune with the world." And lifting her chin, she declared firmly:

"Which I tell him is ridiculous."

"I'm not so sure," said Herbie. "What passes for a tune today sounds to me like so much caterwauling. As that English writer—what's his name?—says, 'Random noise considered as art.' "

"Kingsley Amis," I said. "I'm afraid I agree with him. In all the arts. Random noise, with neither form nor style."

"The revolution," said Herbie gloomily. "To break the forms, overturn the structure. To what end?" He sighed and put down his napkin. "What I should like," he said, "is to take a little stroll after dinner. To settle both my mind and my stomach. There are some things I want to remember—besides Cordelia's excellent meat loaf. Are we anywhere near the sea?"

"It's just beyond the hill," I said. "I'll go with you."

"Good," said Herbie. "We'll walk along the shore together and talk." He paused, as though struck by a sudden thought. "You know, Bobby," he said, "it's been a long while since we've talked to each other."

I didn't say what I wanted to say: that he had been ill for some time and that my last memories of York included my standing with Ruth in the kitchen of the great house, hearing Herbie in his bedroom upstairs roaring for her to bring him his breakfast without delay. "He gets so impatient these days," Ruth had said helplessly, filling his tray with everything she could find.

I remember that I watched in amazement as she carried off to him some cold asparagus and a plate of lobster bisque left over from the night before.

"The tide will be going out," I said and, rising, bent over to kiss Cordelia's cool cheek. "You don't mind?" I asked.

"Of course not. It's a lovely idea."

"Very well. Come along, then, Admiral."

"Admiral?" Herbie asked in surprise and then laughed suddenly. "I haven't heard that in years."

Chapter 5

IT was a full moonlight night and the sea lay spread before us, darkly shining under the paler night-blue sky. The surf broke in dim, white, wavering lines out in the darkness and hissed in toward us in silvery foam; sand and shingle scrunched under our feet. "The grunion are running," I said. "We should have brought a pail."

"Grunion?" asked Herbie. "What are they? Some fearsome trolls from an ocean elf-land?"

I told him that they were small fish, rather transparent, gelatinous, like squid; that at each season, under the full moon, they rushed up onto the beaches to spawn and—if they missed the receding tide—to die; and that people came to the shore with buckets and pails to gather them up.

"So many forms of life," mused Herbie, "and the
same end for all. Or is it? The self . . . does the whatever-
it-is—the grunion—know itself to be an individual? Is
it, actually, an individual? Or the honeybee? Does the
crab have a self? And can there be a self without memory?
At what point does the living form acquire memories?"

"The bee," I said, "remembers where she has been
and informs her sisters by means of a ritualistic dance."

"Ah," said Herbie; "but does she remember it
tomorrow? Pavlov's salivating dogs remembered the
ringing of a bell, but did they remember their childhood?
Memory is more than a conditioned response; it moves
in another field. I can remember to eat my pudding with
a spoon, but something else in me remembers joy and
sorrow."

The moon, still rising, floated behind us in the east;
far to the west above the water a single star hung small
and silver in the sky. For a moment I was back in
Cambridge, with César Franck's lonely flute sounding
in my ears. I sang the phrase softly to myself.

"What's that?" asked Herbie.

"The Franck. Don't you remember?"

"No," said Herbie.

"It was a path to somewhere once," I said.

"Somewhere?"

"The world."

"The world seems far away to me, Bobby," he said. "Men and their affairs. That's hard for a historian. I try to remember."

"Try harder," I urged. "Go back."

"When I go back," he said, "I find only anger. And fright."

"There was more," I said.

"Was there?" He sounded weary and sad. "I don't remember."

There were others on the beach, shadowy figures in the moonlight, gathering up the silvery fish; their voices mingled with the sound of the waves. One such figure approached us, carrying a large bag; as he drew near, I recognized Mr. Mortimer the antiquarian. "Ah," he said; "there you are." As though he had expected to find us there.

"I didn't know you were a fisherman too," I said.

He smiled and stooped to pick up a grunion. It lay quite still in his hand, and he turned it over, not, I thought, without sympathy. "It is of no further use to itself," he observed. "Already, in its way, it is an antique."

I pointed out that it was still useful in a pot or on a griddle, to which Mr. Mortimer assented gravely. "All living things take nourishment from the dead," he declared. "You should know, being a writer."

He paused, noticing my expression. "Does it surprise

you to find that I know who you are?" he asked. "A
very simple matter, really: I had only to inquire. You
are fairly well known hereabouts. I always like to seek
out the circumstances of the people whose homes I visit."

"I see," I said a bit stiffly. "Then you know that when
I told you that I had nothing of value . . ."

He held up his hand reprovingly. "Everyone has
something of value," he said and popped the grunion
into his bag. I thought that his glance strayed a moment
toward Herbie and that he was about to address him, but
apparently thought better of it. "Yes," he said, "we live
on the past; we are nourished by history."

I saw Herbie's look of surprise—rather pleased
surprise, I thought. But when he spoke, his tone was
bitter. "Young people today do not think so," he said.

"In time," said Mr. Mortimer, "they grow older. I
dare say that you yourself, when young . . ."

"We were all revolutionaries," said Herbie, "in our
time. But not like today. We tried to learn from the past,
not to sweep it under the rug. To build on it, not to wipe
it out as though it had never been."

"One cannot wipe out the past," said Mr. Mortimer.
"It is there. One has only to look back, and there it is.
One learns that in the antique business."

And slinging his bag full of dead fish over his

shoulder, he turned away. "I shall see you again," he
said.

Herbie gazed after him with a curious expression on
his face. "A strange fellow," he said, "and rather too
friendly. Still—what he said about looking back . . ."

He drew a deep breath and frowned. "Damn it,
Bobby," he said, "I wish I knew where I was going." He
kicked moodily at the sand underfoot. "It's extremely
irritating of Ruth not to have been more specific." He
sighed deeply. "She has been irritating," he admitted,
"for as long as I can remember."

"The trouble," I said, "is with your memory."

"I remember a lot of things," he said stubbornly.
"And most of them sour my stomach. All those years in
Washington . . ."

He waved them away in disdain. "But this journey,"
he said. "I confess, I don't remember where I'm supposed
to be. Or even if my passport is in order."

He shivered suddenly in the cold night air. "There's
a little café down the beach a bit," I said. "How about
a cup of coffee to warm us?"

"Coffee?" He made a scornful noise. "Brandy,
rather."

"Larry writes," I began, "that the doctors have told
you . . ."

"All medicines are poison," said Herbie. "What the doctors do is measure one poison against another. The shamans of the Stone Age, the witch doctors of Neolithic times, used curare to both kill and cure. My poison is brandy, so was Churchill's. Neither of us could abide doctors."

He smiled suddenly and sweetly. "Except Larry, of course," he said gently. "I shall miss Larry. But then—he never stuck needles into me. Those damn needles . . ."

The café, situated on a fishing pier a few hundred yards down the beach, had—as it turned out—no license to serve hard liquor, and we were obliged to make do with coffee after all. A small combo was at work in the café: three long-haired, ragged, barefoot young men, two with guitars and one with a set of drums. Their voices, flower-soft, high-pitched, uncertain, might have been the voices of young black girls, knowing and precocious. There was no discernible tune; to the accompaniment of two alternating chords on the guitars and the thump-rattle of the drums, they wailed in the night.

"I have no ear for music," said Herbie, "but I wish they would stop."

"What you are hearing," I told him, "is Soul."

"Soul?" He stared at the singers with a mixture of

surprise and incredulity. "What makes it Soul?" he asked.

"It is African," I said lamely. "Or at least, it's supposed to be."

He shook his head in disagreement. "I've traveled extensively for the State Department," he said, "both in Africa and in the Middle East, and I can assure you that what I'm hearing is purely Byzantine.

"Besides," he said, "I don't like it."

A young man sitting near us, and dressed in nothing but a ragged pair of trousers, leaned across his table toward us. "Man," he said, "that song is about a young girl who died from too many downers. Like it is very beautiful and puts the blame where it belongs."

"And where is that?" asked Herbie.

"Like on society," said the young man.

"I see," said Herbie. "Naturally, that makes sense."

I could tell that he was beginning to enjoy himself in a sarcastic way and that it would all end up in a row. "Herbie," I said, "what you are listening to is the most popular sound in the world today."

"Good God!" he said.

"Young girls," I said, "are attracted to this sound like wasps to honey. It excites them almost to the point of ecstasy, but they remain virgins. They are safe, in the audience."

45

"I'm glad I'm an old man," said Herbie, "and don't have to listen to it."

The young man, with nothing on above his belt except a string of beads around his neck, rose slowly to his feet. "You listen to it," he said, "but you don't hear it."

"I wish," said Herbie dryly, "that I did not."

"You're listening for yesterday," said the young man. "What you want is lollipops. Like there's a tomorrow with the sun shining on it. Jesus!"

"What I don't want," said Herbie, "is rudeness."

"Oh wow!" said the young man.

I half rose from my chair, wanting to intervene, but sat down again. After all, I was no match for a young savage dressed in jeans and a string of beads. Neither was Herbie, but he didn't seem to care.

"Like I say," the young man went on, "there's no place anymore for yesterday. It's dead, man. It stinks up today."

Herbie sniffed audibly in the young man's direction. "Does it?" he inquired. "I thought it was something else."

"What's more," he added, pointing to the combo busily sawing away at their instruments, "I don't like noise."

The young man glanced back at the musicians. "Those

are beautiful people," he said slowly. "You don't want
to go insulting them. I tell you, yesterday is dead, man.
It's garbage."

"Without yesterday," said Herbie coldly, "you
wouldn't be here. So you can count yourself dead as
well."

"Maybe I am dead," said the young man. "Maybe
we all are." In a slow, almost trancelike motion, he drew
a slender knife out of his waistband and, holding it up
in front of his face, stared at it with curiously hungry
eyes. "Maybe the whole world is garbage," he said and
wiped his mouth with the back of his hand.

"Let me tell you . . ." Herbie began.

"You can't tell me anything," said the young man,
"because you're nowhere. Like you're not here."

He turned the point of his knife ever so slowly
toward Herbie's neck. "Are you dead, man?" he asked
softly. "Are you dead? Oh wow!"

I would never have thought that I'd be thankful to
see my friend the antique dealer again, but at that
moment I was. He came in through the door and up to
the young man with the knife and emptied his bag of
fish over him. "Not yet," he said. "Not here."

The cascade of silvery fish threw the young man off
balance; he stared about him for a moment with his
mouth open, and then, suddenly realizing that grunion

were edible—that they were, in fact, bread, he put away his knife, seized the bag, and stooped to gather them up off the floor. We also rose and quietly followed Mr. Mortimer out of the café.

"Mark, 6:42," I said. " 'And they did eat and were filled.' The miracle of the fishes."

"If it amuses you to think so," said the antique dealer.

"What I detest," said Herbie, "is arrogance. As though a knife were a cause for pride."

"What else has he to be proud of?" I asked. "A necktie?"

"Real pride rules out arrogance," said Herbie. "If a man has pride, he doesn't need a knife. That's the trouble with people nowadays: arrogance. A lot of Barbary apes. How about that brandy now?"

"I have a very good Martel," said Mr. Mortimer. "If you'd care to visit my van. It's quite nearby."

"Splendid!" cried Herbie. "You saved my life once—you shall save it again."

"In that case," said Mr. Mortimer, "if you will just follow me . . ."

Chapter 6

THE antiquarian's van proved rather a surprise, for
once inside it appeared to be much larger than I would
have thought. The walls were hung with pictures,
colored prints, framed documents, photographs; many of
the documents and prints struck me, at first glance, as
being valuable and even rare. Three cabinets and a
glass-topped showcase were stuffed with objects of
undoubted antiquity, among which I recognized a copy
of the Venus of Willendorf, that earliest image of the
female form; a bear carved from an ivory tusk; and the
mask of a Chinese warrior. Illumination came from the
ceiling which was painted to represent a night sky from
which small lights like stars gleamed on the walls and
the cabinets.

Seeing me standing lost in admiration in front of
what was obviously a very old and very beautiful sword,
Mr. Mortimer moved to my side. "That is the sword of
Ambrosius Aurelius," he said, "Count of Britain, and
given by him to his son, Arthur, Dux Brittanorum. It
was known by the name of Excalibur."

"Oh, come!" I said.

Mr. Mortimer smiled. "I see that you doubt it," he
said. "Nevertheless, I found it at the bottom of a lake
in Devonshire."

Taking from the showcase a small, parchment-bound
book, he held it out for me to see. "And here," he said,
"are the poems of the Lady Vittoria Colonna who was
as you know the lover of Michelangelo—insofar as
possible."

Moving to one of the cabinets, he showed me a
black stovepipe hat which he claimed to have been
worn by President Lincoln at Ford's Theater on the
night of April 14, 1865. "Over there," he said, "is the
suit of lights worn by Manolete the day he was killed.
And here," holding out to me a small golden object, "is
a button from Lord Nelson's cape."

He shrugged his shoulders disarmingly. "As you see,"
he said, "I take everything."

What an old rascal, I thought, half amused, half
admiring, for there was something about him, swindler

though he certainly was—some simple earnestness, an
innocence almost—that made its way through to me.
I murmured some polite response and turned to find
Herbie staring at a picture on the wall. He seemed
curiously tense, and I went over to see what had
affected him.

It appeared to be an ordinary enough photograph: a
foreign-looking gentleman, slender, with thinning
gray hair, tight lips, and shrewd eyes behind gleaming
rimless spectacles, was seated at what appeared to be a
conference table, along with a group of other gentlemen,
some, from the looks of them, foreigners like himself,
others more familiarly American in appearance. "What
is it, Herbie?" I asked.

"It's the visit of the German delegation to the State
Department," said Herbie in a taut voice, "back in 1933.
That evil-looking fellow in the eyeglasses is Hjalmar
Schacht, Hitler's Minister of Finance."

He pointed with his finger to a figure in the corner.
"That's me," he said. "And there's Bullitt and Warburg
and Senator Key Pittman."

He took a deep breath. "The son of a bitch had just
told us that Germany wasn't going to pay her debts," he
said. "Not only told us—but with such arrogance . . .

"God, Bobby! How it brings it all back. The
heartsickness, watching a world going to pieces. And

not being able to do anything about it. And the devil is, it's all forgotten now, the lies, the slogans, the ever-rising madness. 'Tomorrow the world' . . ."

He stopped suddenly. "Where the devil did this fellow ever get that picture?" he demanded. "I don't remember any photographer . . ."

"He has some odd things," I said.

"Damn it," he cried, "those aren't the things I want to remember."

"What do you want to remember, Admiral?"

He shook his head. "I don't know," he said sadly. "Whatever it is, I can't remember it."

I thought of his long struggle within the State Department to stockpile the materials needed for the war he knew—and so few believed—was coming: his battle for rubber, his search for oil, for tin, for time . . . all in the gray cloud of indecision which hung like a fog over Washington and Whitehall. . . .

"There were no pineapples in it," I said.

"Pineapples?" He turned a puzzled face to me. "Pineapples?" His face broke into a rueful smile. "By God," he said, "I'd forgotten."

He shook his head sadly. "No," he said. "There were no pineapples anywhere."

He sank wearily into a chair in front of the picture. "How often," he said, "I used to come home after a day

of evasions, of stupidities, of politics-as-usual, and turn
my anger on Ruth, who was there and available."

"She loved you anyway," I said.

"I know. And I loved her too . . . I suppose. In a way.
But there were times when I was happier alone.

"Until this last time," he said softly. And he added
in an uncertain voice;

"I think I miss her."

"Well, now," said Mr. Mortimer coming up to us
with a tray on which he had arranged a bottle and
three glasses, "here is the brandy I promised you.
Martel, 1810 . . . as you can see. And here," handing
him a very large cigar, "is one of Mr. Churchill's
favorite coronas."

Herbie took it almost absentmindedly. "I remember,"
he said, "that night, after the meeting, we went out to
dinner at a restaurant, and the waiter was rude. I think
he was a German. Or maybe not . . . it doesn't matter.
Anyway, I ordered something, and he brought us
something else. Ruth didn't want to say anything, but
I damned him up and down and walked out. She never
wanted to say anything. . . ."

That the brandy was as old as Mr. Mortimer said was
of all things the most unlikely, but it was curiously
warming. It seemed to relax Herbie; after a few swallows,
he sighed comfortably and leaned back in his chair. "We

53

had a house in Geneva once," he said. "You were there,
weren't you?"

"Yes," I said. "And Larry and his wife. It was a good
time."

"Was it?" said Herbie.

He was silent, his face turned up to the night sky
painted on the ceiling; he seemed to be staring somberly
into the past. I took a sip of my brandy; I was obliged
to admit that I had never tasted a better. Mr. Mortimer
nodded and winked at me, and I raised my glass to him
by way of compliment.

"To all journeys," he said. "May they turn home in
peace."

As we sat there in comfortable silence, there was a
knock on the van door, and Mr. Mortimer went to open
it. A man stood there, dressed in the habit of a preacher,
a Christian minister, but of what denomination I could
not tell. He had a book in his hand, which he held out
to the antique dealer. "They say you buy old books," he
said hesitantly, "and I thought you might like to buy this
one."

Mr. Mortimer took it and examined it carefully. "I
see," he said, "that you have a copy of Archbishop
Parker's 'Treacle Bible,' published in 1586. It is rare
and worth more than I could afford. A museum or
library would pay you more for it."

Cocking his head to one side, he looked at his visitor curiously. "But tell me," he said, "why should you want to get rid of such a treasure?"

The visitor hung his head; he appeared ill at ease, shuffled his feet, and had some difficulty deciding what to say. "To be honest," he said at last, "I do not believe in it anymore. 'Lord, I believe; help Thou my unbelief.' The Kingdom of God is *not* at hand, and the meek do not inherit the earth. When I preach Christ the Savior to the poor and the afflicted, I feel like a hypocrite."

Mr. Mortimer nodded understandingly. "Still," he said, "they get comfort from it."

"Ah," said the minister bitterly, "but I do not."

"Well," said Mr. Mortimer gently, "I cannot buy your book. But I can sell you one of even greater value for practically nothing."

"Why would you do that?" asked the minister, startled.

The antiquarian smiled. "I am not in this business to make money," he said. "I am here because of my interest in people."

He went to one of the cabinets and removed a roll of papyrus. "I have here," he said, "an ancient scroll. It is older than the earliest fragments of papyrus containing bits of the New Testament. It was discovered in a cave near the Dead Sea. It is four hundred years older than the Codex Sinaiaticus. It is the story of Jesus."

"Of Christ?" exclaimed the minister incredulously. "The Son of God?"

"No," said Mr. Mortimer. "It is the story of Jesus, the Son of Man. The Christ was Paul's idea."

Seeing the preacher turn color at this, Mr. Mortimer went on quickly.

"It is much harder to be the son of man, than to be the Son of God. Even the sparrow is God's child, even the lily of the field. But the son of man has a heavy cross to bear. Surrounded by mystery, subject to mortal doubt, he must comfort his people."

"Are you trying to tell me," said the preacher, "that Jesus was not sent to redeem the world from sin?"

Mr. Mortimer made a conciliatory gesture with his hands. "Be reasonable," he said. "To a Jew, to sin was to depart from the strict observance of the Law. To lay the sins of all mankind on Jesus' shoulders was purely Paulian. No, my friend. Jesus was a great and holy man, touched like Buddha by the divine spirit, but he was also, first and foremost, a revolutionary. The Jews had been promised a Messiah, who was to redeem Israel from her enemies and transform her into God's favorite kingdom once again. This, as you know, Jesus did not do, and the Jews turned him over to the Romans as a failed Messiah."

"But you do believe," insisted the preacher, "that God manifested Himself in Jesus?"

"Certainly," replied Mr. Mortimer, "I believe that He manifests Himself in all things. Even in me."

And pressing the scroll into the other's hands, he remarked:

"Here, take it and pay me what you can. It will not tell you what you would like to know about the future in heaven, but it will teach you what you ought to know about the past on earth."

Confused and troubled, the preacher took the scroll and turned away. But he had not been gone for more than a minute, when he was back again. "I cannot read this book," he declared in an agitated voice. "It is in a strange language."

"Naturally," said Mr. Mortimer. "It is in Aramaic, the language of the streets. The disciples were humble men; it was the language Jesus spoke himself, and a friend, writing about him, would naturally use it. I say 'humble men,' but in fact, Simon and Judas were Zealots."

The preacher hurried off, the scroll clutched to his breast.

"I am surprised," said Herbie to Mr. Mortimer when the door had closed on him, "to find you such a biblical scholar. Obviously the Gospels weren't written by historians; there's no mention in either Matthew, Mark, or Luke of the political climate of the period. One would expect at least something about the Occupation, the opposition of liberal and conservative forces, the rise of a Third Party. Besides, the Jews of 30 B.C. were not so much interested in a heavenly kingdom as in an earthly one—if one excepts the Chassidic Essenes—and they have remained so to this day. Actually, one could call Ben-Gurion the real Messiah—though no one has done so."

"You have done so now," I said. "However, there is one more thing; the little matter of the Resurrection."

"When Jesus reappeared after his death," said Mr. Mortimer, "his disciples failed to recognize him."

Herbie shrugged his shoulders. "After all," he said, "while he was still alive, Peter denied him three times. It is not always politic to recognize a condemned man. As an official of the State Department, I learned to distrust both the oral and the written word."

He moved moodily in his chair. "But after all," he remarked, "what has this to do with a lonely man on a journey? I am beginning to feel cold again. Let us go home."

Chapter 7

Herbie continued the conversation on the way home.
"I feel a great sympathy for that poor preacher, Bobby,"
he said. "I too would have liked to find my comfort in
Christ. Because Christianity, as announced by Paul, and
later affirmed by Matthew, Mark, and Luke, brought a
new hope into the world, promising repose in heaven
and peace on earth. However, the history of Paul's
church is not edifying. And I fear that the young and
eager Jesus-seekers of today may end up no less bigoted
and violent than their ancestors."

"On the other hand—" I began.

"I know," said Herbie testily. "I know: that unpleasant
young man with the knife may turn out to be the

grandfather of tomorrow's Galileo. It is true that the
rude and riotous behavior of the students of the
universities of Bologna, Padua, and Toledo helped bring
about the end of the Dark Ages and the beginnings of
the Renaissance. Nevertheless, for the taxpayers of the
Middle Ages, it must have been extremely irritating. We
cannot look ahead with certainty, simply because in the
past we have somehow managed to muddle through.
There have been many periods when mankind seemed
headed for the lunatic asylum; we may not escape it
altogether. The more I see—and hear—the work of our
artists, the more I listen to our thinkers, the less convinced
I am that we shall escape it at all."

The night stood over us in a great bowl, stretching
away above our heads to infinity. Beyond the blue,
moonlit air lay the eternal darkness . . . the same
darkness that had stood above us long ago on Harvard
Bridge, that had stood over the Greeks at Marathon, the
reed ships of the Egyptians, the wars of Gilgamesh, the
death of the last dinosaur, and the birth of Jesus.

" 'If we cling,' " Herbie quoted, " 'to this little station
above the endless waters, it is because that is all we have
to cling to: the yellow flower of day, the rose of evening.'
Do you recognize that, Bobby?"

"I'm not sure," I said. "It sounds a little like me . . .
that yellow flower of day—but . . ."

"It's you all right," said Herbie gleefully. "And you don't know what it's from?"

"I don't remember."

He nodded, satisfied to have caught me out. "Here's something else," he said, " 'This is man's life and of his life the whole, this yellow light of day, this little rose. . . .' "

But this time I recognized my own sonnet. " 'This little heaven that we call the earth,' " I quoted, " 'is made to bloom by kindness and men's love—' "

He added the last line. " 'But only once,' " he said, " 'that I have knowledge of.' " He stood still, staring up at the night. "Once," he said, half to himself. "Only once."

Turning to me, he added almost casually:

"Your antiquarian friend obviously doesn't believe in heaven. I suppose you don't, either. . . ."

It was left in the air in the form of a question, and I answered with another. "Do you mean the Christian heaven or merely some form of life hereafter?"

He shook his head in a puzzled way. "Frankly, Bobby," he said, "I don't know. I never gave it much thought before. But lately . . ."

"Admiral," I said firmly, "I am an ignorant three dimensional being in a fourth- or fifth- or even seventh-dimensional universe. If I believe in anything, it is in my own ignorance. And as a matter of fact, I get all the comfort I need from just that, from not thinking that I know the answers. I'm sure there is some great mystery of which I am a part, that there is a Creator simply because there is a creation. After all, nothing comes from nothing. That such a Creator actually made man in His own image seems to me extremely unlikely, when one considers the work of Dr. Leakey and other anthropologists; that He chose Abraham to be His sole witness, defies reason. Yet our Judaeo-Christian religion with its heaven and hell is based upon just such statements.

"On the other hand, I am aware of a life of the spirit which is nonresponsive to our own bodies, a life—if life it can be called—of the mind, of the self, curiously independent of the brain. That is as far as I am willing to go: that there is another dimension. That we enter that mysterious world with our own sense of self, with all our memories, I very much doubt; that we cease to exist in any dimension, I doubt even more. But in what form, or with what memories we persist, I do not know. What I hope, of course, is another matter."

"And what do you hope, then?"

"Simply," I said, "to die happy."

I knew that I had expressed myself poorly; that what

I really meant was that I wanted my last thoughts to be a celebration of life, that I wanted to die in the awareness of love, and that there was no way that I could say this to Herbie without seeming to reproach him with his marriage.

We returned home as we had come, by way of the beach. The tide was out now, but there were still a few people on the shore, searching for the last of the limp, silver bodies; vague figures among the rocks, they appeared and disapppeared in the moon-mist. It was all shadowy, veiled; halfway down the beach we came on a young girl, a child, crouched with her pail in the sand under the loom of a kelp-covered boulder. "Whoops!" exclaimed Herbie gaily. "We've all but stepped on a small octopus!"

There was the tiniest giggle from the sand. "I'm not an octopus," said the child.

"Well, then," Herbie insisted, "you're a mermaid."

"I'm not neither."

She might have been six or seven. "Look," she said and held up her pail half full of fish.

"Why," said Herbie in mock surprise, "you're a fisherman."

"I got a whole lot," she said proudly. And she added sympathetically:

63

"Don't you have any?"

Herbie shook his head sadly. "You see," he said solemnly, "we keep putting them back in the ocean."

"Oh," she said. "But that's silly. Why?"

He was in a teasing mood; there was obviously something about the little girl that took him back to a faraway long-ago childhood. "You see," he said gravely, "they asked us to."

She gazed somewhat doubtfully at her pail. "They didn't neither," she said, but her voice lacked conviction.

He bent down and took the little girl's pail and peered into it. "I'm sorry," he said to the slither of fish inside. "Clara and Tommy and Miranda, the little girl is going to eat you all up." He gave the pail back to her and smiled down at her in the darkness. "They said all right," he said.

She thought about it for a while, gazing up at him gravely. "I know a secret," she said at last.

"I know a secret too," said Herbie. "What's yours?"

The little girl fumbled in the pocket of her dress and drew out a small conch shell. "I found this on the beach," she said. "It's beautiful."

"So it is," said Herbie dutifully.

"It's the most beautiful thing I ever had," she said. "I'm going to keep it forever and ever.

"I'm never going to forget it."

He took it in his hand and turned it this way and that.

"Will you give it to me?" he asked.

As he stood looking down at her, I was suddenly reminded of the Herbie of long ago, curly-headed, incorrigible. . . . I thought of the time the Harvard Liberal Club had invited H. G. Wells to address its members and had discovered to its horror that Mr. Wells's fee was a thousand dollars. To which Herbie, as president, had cabled back an offer: MAKE IT FIFTY DOLLARS AND A DINNER. He had never received a reply.

He had one now, however. The child drew back not unlike the little octopus he had first named her. "No," she said.

"Please?"

I was afraid he'd frighten her. "Herbie," I said, "really . . ."

He paid no attention to me. "I don't see why not," he said. "After all, you can always remember it."

She put the shell back in her pocket and gazed up at him calmly. "No," she said. And then, being a woman, and curious:

"Why should I?" she demanded.

"Because I have nothing beautiful to remember forever and ever," said Herbie.

"Well," she said slowly, "you can have one of my fishes."

"Thank you," said Herbie.

As we turned away, a woman whom I took to be the little girl's mother came up to join her daughter. "What were they saying to you?" she demanded. "What did they want?"

Oppressed by her mother's anxiety and by the lateness of the hour, the child began to sniffle. "They wanted to take my shell away," she whined.

We were already several yards off and soon to be out of earshot, but not until I heard the mother's voice, thin against the sound of the sea:

"Nothing is safe anymore."

I don't think that he heard her. "Where one's treasure is," he said gently. "A little shell. And she was never going to forget it, ever."

"How do you remember the most beautiful thing in the world, Bobby?"

For a moment, the picture of Cordelia in her garden flashed through my mind. "I don't know," I said, "but you'd better try. Because in the end, that's all you can take."

"Where to?"

I made a vague, helpless gesture. "Ah," I said.

He nodded soberly. "If we knew that," he agreed, "we wouldn't feel so lost. But we don't know, and we can't know, and that's what's frightening."

"I'm not frightened," I told him. "As long as I can't know, there's no use worrying."

"Still," he said, "you can't ignore it altogether. How do you imagine it, Bobby? Obliteration? Nothing?"

He took my silence for disagreement, which it was.

"What else then?"

"Reason," I said slowly, "tells me: nothing. But some sense beyond reason tells me that there is such a thing as spirit—free of the body, free of the brain. I'm not talking about ghosts, about apparitions—or even the 'dear departed' who speak to mediums from 'the other side'; there has always seemed something unreasonable about that. Mysterious, yes—but still, unreasonable. Because 'the other side' seems like such a mirror image of our own. . . . No, there is something else on that other side, something incomprehensible. What it is, I don't know, but I have felt the watchfulness, the lingering concern of more than one lost, loving friend—felt it in some deep part of my spirit, felt it in the air around me, in the quiet room, in the flowering garden. A rose blooming out of season, a butterfly returning . . ."

"Reincarnation?"

"No, that, too, is unreasonable, because time is all around us like a sea, and there is neither a before nor an after."

"Each moment, then, a moment in eternity?"

"Each moment *is* eternity," I said. "Let me work it out for you."

And counting it out on one finger after another, I continued: "The dot, mathematically speaking, has no dimension at all. It is contained in the line, which is the first dimension. The second dimension, which we call the plane, contains the first, while the third contains the second. And the third dimension, which is the cube, and which is all we see of our material universe, is itself contained in time, which we call the fourth dimension. And time rests in eternity . . . do you see what I'm getting at? . . . and eternity rests in infinity. And when we get to the seventh dimension, we come to something that contains them all—the dot, the line, the plane, the cube, time, eternity, and infinity—and we call it God. Or, at least, I do, and I'm convinced that He is as indifferent to me as He is to a caterpillar."

"You're no help to me at all," said Herbie.

Chapter 8

THE lights were still on at my house when we got back, but there was no immediate welcome. Cordelia, who had gone upstairs with a book, had apparently fallen asleep on the bed, waiting for us. "You were gone a long time, darling," she said drowsily when I came in. "Is everything all right?"

"Herbie has gone to bed," I said and began to undress. I felt suddenly very tired.

Cordelia yawned, arching herself like a cat, stretched and sat up, her arms wrapped around her knees. "We had a call," she said. "From Ruth."

"Oh?" I stared at her in surprise. "From Ruth?" I asked. I should have been pleased; now perhaps Herbie would find out where he was supposed to be. But for some reason, my heart skipped a beat, and something inside me turned cold. "What did she say?" I asked.

"It was just after you'd left," said Cordelia. That would have made it nearly midnight in the east. "I told her that he was here, and she didn't say anything. I told her that he'd tried to get through to her, and she said 'thank you' in such a strange, flat voice, and then she said that he wasn't really there anymore, and I said that of course, no, he was here, and she started to cry. . . . It was all so odd, the conversation, it seemed to go in circles."

"Yes," I said.

But later, in bed, she clung to me, her head as usual on my shoulder. "Robbie," she said in a small voice: "I'm frightened."

"Don't be," I said. "Whatever it is."

"That horrible old man," she whispered, "with his horrible van . . ."

"We saw him again," I said. "He isn't horrible at all. As a matter of fact, he's very . . . well, he knows a lot. About all kinds of things. Actually—he sort of came to our rescue. . . ."

Then I had to tell her about the young man in the café, and she sat up suddenly and gazed at me in fright. "You could both of you have been killed or something!" she exclaimed.

She threw herself back on her pillow in exasperation. "It's this awful country," she cried. "I wish we were in England."

"People get killed in England too," I pointed out mildly.

"Not nice people," she said.

God rests once more above Israel. That is to say, Iaveh, the Lord of Hosts, having spent two thousand years diffused above Kiev, Warsaw, Toledo, Cologne, the Trastevere, floats once more above Jerusalem, like a balloon, buoyed upward by the millions of souls who compose His spiritual body. He lies, as it were, eyeball to eyeball with Allah, whose witnesses surround Him on every side; while to the northwest, above St. Peter's, floats the ineffable Trinity, wafted in incense.

What does it mean to be a Jew? I do not follow the dietary laws, pray in the Synagogue, keep the Sabbath, celebrate the Passover, observe the Holy Days, or worship the God of the Bible. I am a Jew because my forefathers were Jews; because my ancestors remained Jews through every possible discouragement. Because their blood is in my veins. They were enormously steadfast; that we differ about the universe is of the least importance.

I see no reason to be either proud or sorry. Although I am a writer, an artist—a poet, even—I am not

ROBERT NATHAN

contemptuous of society, and I do not feel the need to
insult anyone. Like that Voice that spoke to Moses,
I am that I am.

If my ancestors had been cockroaches, I'd have been
a cockroach.

> Men nobler than myself
> Have set me like a tree.
> My roots are in their dust.
>
> My roots are deep, I trust.

In my younger days, the little verse had two more
lines to it, before the last line:

> Let the wind blow!
> What is that to me?

One becomes less defiant of the wind as one grows
older. As for religion—in the year 2012 B.C.—more or
less—many billions of years after the Creation, God
offered Himself to Abraham, a Hebrew living in Ur,
in Chaldea; and for reasons known only to Himself
chose Abraham's descendants to be His witnesses on
earth. It must be said that He dealt with them very
harshly. Three thousand years later they were being

72

burned alive by people professing to worship this same
God, with some changes: He was now a Trinity.

What is one to make of such nonsense? And why
Abraham?

Cordelia, who is wholly Church of England—yet
not altogether wholly, for she is inclined to believe in
reincarnation—often insists that she sees in me a certain
resemblance to the Duke of Wellington. I have, it is true,
a large nose, which turns wet. "All Englishmen," she
says, "have wet noses." No doubt it is the climate.

But to believe in reincarnation is to believe that time
marches on, that it is a progression, with yesterday lost
somewhere behind us and tomorrow waiting on ahead.
"One has lived in the past; one will live again in the
future." It is to ignore the fourth dimension, in which time
literally stands still. In the eternal *now*, one cannot *have
been* anyone else; with my large wet nose, I must believe
myself to be at one and the same time myself, the
Duke—and, for all I know, Solomon and Hammurabi
and my neighbor's dog.

So what do I believe? I believe in my own ignorance,
and I believe in God—a God about Whom I know
nothing. His being is mysterious, His power
incomprehensible, His place in the cosmos unknown.
He gives life to insects and men alike and is equally

indifferent to their welfare. His purposes are inscrutable;
He rests in eternity and in infinity. He is at once now,
then, and always; the Creator of space, of matter, of the
stars, suns, and planets, of the single cell and of Abraham,
and I cannot even imagine Him.

Why do I say "Him"? Is it because, for so long, men
have thought of God as the Father? Yet He must also be
the Mother.

Can I be said to love Him? I know it is the thing to
say. But since I cannot imagine Him, let me say rather
that I love His creation—although it horrifies me at times
by its cruelty. Just the same, I admire its vast design.
And as the poet Max Ehrmann says, I am a child of the
universe and have a right to be here.

So has a gnat. I think that God is equally aware of
us and that we are equally a part of the universe.

This—this profound ignorance—is what, as I tried
to tell Herbie, gives me comfort. For if Iaveh were all
with His irrational fits of temper, or Allah with His
pitiless jihads, or the Trinity with its burnings and
persecutions, I should feel myself no more distinct than
a grunion.

Whereas, on the contrary, I have a most marvelous
sense of self. Where it comes from, I do not know; my
hope is that when I die, that sense of self will not

disappear, but that I shall take it with me. And I want it to be filled with joy. With joy and love: for that is the greatest gift of all.

As long as Cordelia is there with me at the end.

Chapter 9

WE slept and woke. The moon was down, it was the deepest part of the night, but a sea fog had drifted in, giving a milky quality to the darkness, and Herbie, Cordelia, and I went out into it.

It was an odd, dreamlike night in which we found ourselves. There was mist over everything, changing whatever was familiar into something strange, hiding the known, causing trees, bushes, houses to disappear, dissolve, melt away. The road which ran in front of our own house was no longer there . . . or had we somehow missed it? Crossed it without knowing? Where we were appeared to be a wide and empty field, shrouded in mist . . . unrecognizable. "I don't like this," said Cordelia. And looking around anxiously, she added:

"Where are we going?"

"If Ruth had only told me," Herbie grumbled. "But she's grown so muddleheaded."

What struck me most of all was the silence. It was eerie: complete and utter. There was no sound of any sort around us, no night stirrings, no murmur—however faint—of the sea, no distant whisperings of cars along the highway. "Let's go back, Admiral," I said uncomfortably.

"Back to what, Bobby?"

"Let's go home," I said. "Cordelia's cold."

"Dear Cordelia," he said, "forgive me." And turning around, he prepared to start back. "Home," he said. "A great house over a green-flowing river."

He was talking about his own house, in York. "Lilies-of-the-valley," he said, "under the oaks and beeches. Arbutus under the snow and pink and white blossoms in the spring. So many, many rooms . . . the house of an important man. I was never happy there."

"Why, Herbie?" I asked.

"I never felt important enough," he said.

But when we turned back toward the house, or where we thought the house to be, I realized that I was no longer sure of the way—that I was, in fact, completely without sense of direction. "I think we're lost," I said.

"Nonsense, darling," said Cordelia cheerfully. "We

can't possibly be." And peering about through the misty darkness, she suddenly clutched my arm. "Look," she said, pointing: "isn't there a light over there?"

Sure enough, I could make out a faint flicker of light in the distance, and after a moment's hesitation—since it seemed to be in the opposite direction from where I imagined our house to be—we started toward it. However, as we drew near, it turned out to be not a house at all, but a dilapidated motor trailer with the words HODD'S CIRCUS in faded paint along its side. A small fire of chips and dead branches was burning in front of it, and it was this which we had glimpsed in the darkness.

An old iron kettle hung from a tripod above the fire, and, beside it, stirring its contents with a large wooden paddle, stood a clown. He wore a much-dented high hat, the remains of what was once a full-dress suit, the usual oversize shoes, the red, bulbous nose, and that joy to children, the clown's painted grimace of despair.

"Robbie!" exclaimed Cordelia happily, "it's a circus! How lovely!"

"It's a very small circus," I said. But I was surprised to find it there at all. Only Herbie seemed indifferent.

"We seem to have lost our way," he said to the clown. "Can you tell us where to find the road?"

The clown bobbed his head in the old-fashioned

manner of the poor and the humble. "What road would that be, sir?" he asked.

Herbie shrugged his shoulders. "Why, any road at all," he said. To which I added, "The coast road. The road to town."

"There's no such road," said the clown.

"Nonsense," said Herbie sharply. "There has to be. Else how would I be here?"

"Ah," said the clown, peering into the kettle, "now there you have me. How indeed?"

"I tell you, there was a road," said Herbie stubbornly, "and I was on it."

"Were you?" asked the clown meekly. "Then, sir, tell me where it brought you."

"That," said Herbie, "is what I want to know."

"Well, sir," said the clown, "that's hard to tell. I might say that it brought you to the ragtag end of a circus and the universal soup, but that would be clownish of me."

"But you are a clown," said Cordelia, "aren't you?"

"Not by nature, ma'am," he replied. "I've known grander times."

"So have I," said Herbie glumly.

"When I took joy in my work," said the clown. "When my act had wings."

"We all had wings once, Mr. Hodd," said Cordelia

sympathetically. "When we were young."

"Yes ma'am," he said deferentially and then added abruptly, "Call me Luke."

"You're not Hodd?" I asked.

He shrugged carelessly. "I use the name sometimes," he said, "but I like mine better."

"Luke," I said. "The third Synoptic."

It was Cordelia who thought of Lucifer, not I. If it had occurred to me, I'd have been embarrassed to say it, but Cordelia was always more forthright. "I don't think he means that Luke, darling," she said. "I think he means the Devil."

The clown gazed reflectively into the kettle, slowly stirring whatever it was he was cooking, before replying:

"There are many names for the Devil, ma'am, and Lucifer is one of them. But it is ill-used, for it means Light, not Darkness. When Lucifer was cast down, he fell like a flaming comet through the heavens."

"I know," said Cordelia. "I never thought of him as a clown."

"He had no choice," said Luke. "In a world so full of hate, so wild with violence, what else could he be? Even an archangel can't compete with man in brutality."

"Indeed not," said Cordelia. "It's rather sad. Poor Lucifer."

Luke cleared his throat. "You're very kind," he said. "Have some soup."

"Thank you," said Cordelia. "Though actually I don't really think I care for soup at this time. I'd much rather tea, if you have it."

Luke smiled happily. "Splendid," he said. "Now I shall be able to show you one of my clown routines. A bit of magic, you might say." And clapping his hands sharply, he called out to whoever—or whatever—was inside his trailer.

"Tea, please. For four."

At once a pretty young woman appeared from the shadowy interior of the van. Dressed in the uniform of a Victorian parlor maid, she carried a large silver tray on which was arranged a complete silver tea service. She was followed by another, younger girl, bearing a tray of jams, crumpets, small cakes, and watercress sandwiches. A small but elegant tea-table was also brought out, and chairs set up, and after setting the two trays on the table, the young women withdrew, not forgetting to execute a bobbing curtsy to the clown and to ourselves.

"Will you pour, ma'am?" he asked Cordelia, who was already exclaiming—somewhat greedily, I thought—over the jams and jellies. "Fortnum and Mason," she said. "Lovely."

"I must say," I remarked, "you live very well."

Luke nodded happily. "I see," he said, waving a watercress sandwich at me, "that you've noticed my early Georgian teapot, and my nineteenth-century household help. I'm not surprised, for I thought you would, due to your resemblance to the Duke of Wellington."

"They do look a bit alike, don't they?" said Cordelia with satisfaction.

"Look," said Herbie suddenly, "shouldn't we be getting on? After all, we are looking for a road. . . ."

At this Luke rose, made a clown's face, and executed a double somersault. "You're quite right," he said, "it is all my fault; as usual, I have allowed my pride to interfere in human affairs. However, in self-defense, I might add that the point I wished to make was that clowns, like angels, fools, and novelists, are able to evoke the most attractive images of the past."

Herbie looked thoughtful. "Tell me, Mr. Luke," he said, "or Lucifer . . ."

"I never said I was Lucifer," said the clown quickly.

"Just the same," said Herbie, "those housemaids have given me an idea. Can you really summon up such images of the past?"

Luke—or Lucifer—gazed at Herbie thoughtfully for a moment before replying. "As a historian," he said at last, "you must know that the past is not always amiable. It is one thing to bring back for your wife's sake, the England of Victoria, while managing to exclude at the same time the Crimean War, the Boer War, the Black Hole of Calcutta, and the fall of Khartoum. But to evoke the Rome of Vespasian while keeping out the destruction of Jerusalem is not so easy. In fact, it isn't easy at all.

"No—it takes quite a bit of doing, and I'm not always able to control things. Horror comes crowding in; there's so much of it around. . . ."

We were silent; even Cordelia had nothing to say. The fire had died down to a few lingering coals, leaving the night darker around us, and the clown and his trailer had begun to fade into the prevailing gloom. I could no longer see him very clearly; his voice, too, had grown fainter. "Cruelty," he said, sounding far away, "cruelty! Have you seen Babylon in its glory? Or Dahomey? Did you watch the massacre of the Incas? Were you at Bangladesh?"

"No," said Herbie shortly. "Were you?"

"I was," said the clown, in such a faint, faraway whisper that I wasn't even sure I'd heard him.

But almost at once a confused murmur began to sound around us. It seemed to come from the night itself, from some deep well of darkness: a sound of voices, a wind of cries, growing deeper, coming nearer, the clashing of steel and iron, shouts and groans, exultant calls, and a great sound of weeping. And in the weeping, Luke's voice for the last time, far off and faint:

"I, too, wanted glory."

It was like a great storm coming. All violence was in it, and I knew—I had the terrible knowledge—that if it reached us, we'd be swept away in it, overwhelmed . . . by the past, the true past, the true history of man.

Grasping Cordelia by the hand, I pulled her to her feet. "Out of here!" I exclaimed. "Run for it!"

"I rather thought so," she said.

Herbie was already ahead of us, but moving slowly; we, too, seemed to move awkwardly, held back as in a nightmare by some invisible force, while the storm behind us drew nearer and nearer. It was not only a sound now, but a cloud, a visible cloud, darker than the night itself, a black cloud. . . .

"Run," I cried. "Run."

"I can't go any faster," groaned Herbie. I felt Cordelia falter at my side. We were running all out and making no headway. "Darling," cried Cordelia between gasps, "the cloud . . . it's so black. . . ."

"I know," I said. And I did know: I knew that if there was evil in Light, there was greater evil in Darkness. And I knew, too, that there was no shelter for us, that no matter how we ran, we had nowhere to run to.

For in the storm which boiled behind us, I heard all the violence of earth: the rising of the waters of hate, the keening of the winds of mischief, the gathering of the tribes, the fall of kings, the dissolution of empires.

Herbie stumbled to his knees; I grasped him under one arm and Cordelia held him by the other, and we got him to his feet. The ground rose in a gentle slope in front of us, but rough and uneven; slipping, stumbling, we struggled up the rise and over it—and there, below us, was the road, and beside it a service station with its neon lights flooding the night; and in front of it, as though waiting for us, Mr. Mortimer's horse-drawn van.

He came to meet us, beckoning us to hurry. "Man," I cried, "am I glad to see you!"

I thought I caught the flicker of a smile on his face. "There's a horrible storm coming," said Cordelia. "We were almost lost in it."

"I know," said Mr. Mortimer. Opening the door of his van, he bowed us into it. "You'll be all right in here," he said, and following us in, he took his seat on the driver's bench and picked up the reins. "Giddap," he said to his patient old horse, and we set off at a gentle trot.

Flooded with relief, I sank into one of Mr. Mortimer's

antique chairs. Herbie was sitting glumly in a corner, but Cordelia stood in the center of the van looking all around her with an expression of incredulity. "Why," she breathed. "It's a museum!"

Mr. Mortimer nodded his head complacently. "Yes, ma'am," he allowed. "I told you I was a collector."

"But this!" she exclaimed. "I had no idea. You must have everything in the world, right here!"

"I mostly have," he admitted. "Some good pieces, some bad. Not all in plain sight, either."

"Really!" said Cordelia. And she added in wonder, "It's so small, actually—this van, I mean. And yet . . ."

"I know," said Mr. Mortimer. "What you're thinking of are those great houses of England all full of antiques."

"How did you know that?" she asked.

"You'd be surprised how much I know," said Mr. Mortimer.

I could see that Cordelia's natural spirits were returning; there was a little pink in her cheeks, and her chin was pointing upward. "All right," she said, "then tell me: with whom were we having tea just now, before the storm?"

Mr. Mortimer shrugged his shoulders. "That's easy," he said. "It was old Luke. Lucifer, we call him. The spirit that denies . . . and a bit of a clown. Though you can't rightly say he denies; I'd liefer call him a rebel against the Establishment. He gets his bit in now and then, but sooner or later he loses control, and for a while there's all hell to pay. Until the storm blows itself out, and then the Establishment takes over again. Always has, and always will.

"In the end, there has to be Authority."

"Authority," said Herbie rousing himself. "Yes. The dream of brotherhood? There is no brotherhood in men. I was in government; I know."

"It was dreadful," said Cordelia. "Such a feeling of terror. If you hadn't been where you were . . ." She broke off in a puzzled way. "Whatever were you doing," she asked, "at a service station?"

"Why to be sure," said Mr. Mortimer, "gasoline contributes a great deal to my business. Next to wars and the Church . . ."

"I was afraid I'd be killed," said Cordelia. "And I did so want to die in England rather than here."

"Well, so you may," said Mr. Mortimer, "if it matters."

"Of course it matters!" She gave him a long, cool, English look. "You don't care very much for mankind, do you?" she said.

"No," Mr. Mortimer admitted, "I don't. They're a

quarrelsome beast, black, yellow, and white. I was rather fond of the American Indian. . . . However, it's not for me to say, really. I'm a collector, not a judge. Which reminds me: I've got to stop at a house a little ways up the road here, to pick up something . . . that is, if you don't mind. . . ."

Chapter 10

THE house we stopped at was known to me: it was the home of Professor and Mrs. Fineman—or had been, for the professor had died three days before, and the mourning band was still attached to the door. Although not close friends, we had been acquainted with the Finemans, enough to have sent Mrs. Fineman the usual condolences. She received us now in the library; a small, erect, lonely figure, holding an urn in her hands. If she was surprised to see Cordelia, Herbie, and myself, it was obvious that she had been expecting Mr. Mortimer. "Here," she said, holding the urn to him, "this is what you asked for."

Mr. Mortimer took the urn and placed it carefully

ROBERT NATHAN

under his arm. "Are you all right, ma'am?" he asked
kindly.

"As all right," she said, "as might be expected. After
forty years, it is not so easy."

"We know," said Cordelia gently. "But you have so
much to remember. So much that was happy."

"Happy?" asked Mrs. Fineman. "Yes . . . no . . . who
knows? For forty years . . . a long time. We were
married, we were used to each other."

"And love," said Cordelia.

"Love," said Mrs. Fineman, "yes. What else? For
forty years does one live with a stranger?"

I heard Herbie draw in his breath. "Not," she went
on, "that one repeats every morning the word 'love.'
Rather it is there somewhere in the house, in the linen
closet, under the rug. You do each day the day's work; a
marriage is a marriage. Nobody's life is perfect; no matter
where you look, a clown makes a question, whistles up
a storm. Day in and day out, always with the troubles;
they pile up year after year like dishes in the sink. He
does foolish things, he is not so well organized, so you
organize for him, you do not scream. Does he like you
for that? No, he says, you suffocate him. So he does
still more foolish things."

She looked around the room, almost as though she
were looking for someone. "After a while," she said, "you

don't see a person . . . not like he is any more. Instead, you see worries, mistakes, disappointments . . . not a face. Like he wasn't there."

"I know," Herbie breathed and gave a little groan.

"Only, when he was so sick at the end," she said, "then I felt such pity. A man that had been so full of life, so quick, so easy to quarrel . . . I wish I could only forget how he looked, so pitiful. Thin, with such a lost look in the eyes, like he was saying, 'Where am I going?' "

"Please," said Cordelia, "dear Mrs. Fineman . . ."

"My Fineman," said the widow with a break in her voice. "I will miss him forever. For the rest of my life. Don't ask me was I happy. . . . Not all the time, not every day. Marriage is not a honeymoon; you don't feel at dinner like you did at breakfast. But you are fed. And you do not sleep alone, and in the morning you do not wake up in an empty house. I do not think of troubles; I think of one happy day we had together, because that is what I will take with me through the rest of my life. It is enough, for what there is left; there is not so much time now. When we laughed, we laughed together; when we wept, we held each other. How much more do you want? So now, when I cry, I cry by myself."

"We will cry with you," said Mr. Mortimer. And holding the urn out in front of him, he bowed his head over it. "*Yisgadal*," he intoned, "*v'yiskadash, sh'meh rabbo . . . boruch atoh Adonai . . .* Blessed be Thou, King of the Universe. . . ."

We listened reverently to the age-old beauty of the Kaddish; when it was over, Mrs. Fineman drew a long breath of surprise. "You are Jewish too?" she asked Mr. Mortimer.

"Why not?" said Mr. Mortimer.

"You should stay and eat something," said Mrs. Fineman.

It was getting late, and time to be on our way. But I noticed, when we took our places in the van again, that Cordelia's face wore a troubled expression. When I asked her what she was thinking, she shook her head, but after a moment's meditation, turned toward me in a pleading way.

"Tell me something," she said. "Do I suffocate you?"

I denied it at once. "As a matter of fact," I said, "I am even jealous of your roses."

She smiled at that, although I could see that she wasn't altogether convinced. "Promise me," she said, "that you won't die first.

"Because," she went on, "if you did, I'd want to die too. I wouldn't want to go on without you."

"But then," I said, "there'd be no one left to remember me!"

She thought that over for a moment. "There'd be
your books," she ventured.

"My books?" I had to smile. "When an author dies,"
I said, "his books die with him. Tastes change, my darling.
Of my generation, how many are remembered? and for the
wrong reasons? I can think of a dozen—two dozen—great
names, great in their own day, laid away on the library
shelves, wrapped in lavender—while we welcome the
new crop with the same ecstatic cries."

"And you are to survive because of me?"

"For a little while," I said. "Long enough for me
to feel at home in the hereafter."

She burst into tears. "I hate it," she cried. "And
you're being very horrid."

I consoled her as well as I could without embarrassing
Herbie and Mr. Mortimer.

"The hereafter," said Mr. Mortimer meditatively.
And half-turning in his seat, he inquired, "Do you know
much about it?"

"Well, no," I said. "Do you?"

"Nothing whatever," he replied simply.

"Do you remember," Herbie spoke up, "the first time
we heard *Tod und Verklärung* together? Well,
Bobby—it's like that. Death is like that; I know it. Just
like that. The sickness . . . and then that lovely little

93

memory . . . and then the struggle for breath, the heart pounding, beating itself to death. And then silence and the great rising octaves into the Light . . ."

"The Light?" asked Mr. Mortimer. "You think there is a Light?"

"Yes," said Herbie bravely, "I think so."

"It may be so," said Mr. Mortimer indifferently. "One hears of visions. But as far as I can see, when something comes my way, it stops. In that sense, I suppose one might say that this van *is* the hereafter. But music—no."

"I was thinking of Mrs. Fineman," I said. "I was thinking that she loved her husband and that for her, at least, his spirit was still alive."

Mr. Mortimer turned back to his driving again. "Mrs. Fineman," he said. "Yes. Well. There are not too many loving women in the world."

"I thought that Mrs. Fineman was a very loving woman," said Cordelia.

"Did you?" said Mr. Mortimer noncommittally. "Among the Jews, the loving figure is the mother: the father is either a patriarch or a *schlemiel*. A Jewish mother is guardian angel to her son."

"But I think that's very beautiful," said Cordelia.

"I was talking of a loving woman," said Mr. Mortimer, "not a guardian angel."

He continued: "A loving woman, that is to say, a woman made of love alone, who gives all of herself without asking for a reward either here or in heaven."

"Heaven?" I exclaimed in surprise. "I thought . . ."

"I was speaking metaphorically," said Mr. Mortimer. "The point is that she loves without asking what it is costing her or what she is getting. She is not looking for a bargain. Such a woman is very rare and usually to be found in the Orient or in England."

"That is very sweet of you," said Cordelia. "Thank you."

"It is nothing," said Mr. Mortimer, waving it aside.

We drove on in silence for a while. The night was black around us, but I could sense in the darkness that curious stillness which precedes the dawn. The air, too, was colder and sweeter, and Cordelia shivered and nestled closer to me for warmth. Herbie dozed in his chair; all was quiet, the van's wheels and the steady clop-clop of the horse's hooves were the only sound in the stillness.

Chapter II

THE town was quiet, too, when we got there, the street lights gleaming yellow on the empty, bone-bare pavements, the shops closed and dark, all except the shop of the watchmaker, in front of which we stopped.

Once inside, I was surprised at the great number of clocks which filled every corner of the shop, arranged upon tables, set along shelves, and hanging from the walls. There must have been literally hundreds, and no two of them showed the same time.

While Mr. Mortimer and the watchmaker sat down in a corner to discuss business, Herbie, Cordelia, and I wandered about, examining the various timepieces, some new, many of them antiques, often from the very earliest days of clockmaking. A continuous soft chiming filled the air, as the various clocks struck the hour, often minutes apart from their neighbors; and under it a sound not unlike a humming of endless wheels, cogs, balances, pallets, trains, weights, and springs. It was, I thought, a little like being in a beehive with chimes.

One timepiece in particular fascinated me: marked FRAGILE, DO NOT HANDLE, it was a beautifully enameled apparatus in the form of a merry-go-round whose riders, exquisitely fashioned out of ebony, jade, and alabaster, circled forever around a golden platform inscribed with the signs of the zodiac. Here, seated upon a bear, a dragon, an eagle, a lion, a giraffe, a hyena, an elephant, were tiny riders, white, yellow, black, and red, each in an endless chase of the figure ahead and chased, in turn, by the figures behind. Though what, in the continual circling of the riders, could be called ahead or behind was impossible to make out, since by the time a half circle was completed, whoever had been ahead was behind.

At each hour's striking, the carousel stopped for a moment, and whichever rider found himself closest to the goal, which was a gold ring suspended from a pole, rose for a moment in his seat, waved his arm once, and sat down again.

I watched this apparatus for some time, and I saw that the different tracks did not always run at the same

speed, that positions occasionally changed, and that a
black figure, seated upon a hyena, complete with spear,
buffalo shield and a Cyrano de Bergerac hat with a
plume, was catching up with the eagle and was about
to plunge his spear into the bird's tail feathers.

It was a game, I thought, not unlike musical chairs:
when the clock strikes the hour, any one of them can be
opposite the golden ring. But none can stay there long. I
remembered having seen an apparatus like it in
Switzerland long ago, but much smaller and less
ornamental and with fewer figures. I remembered that
it, too, had been marked TRÈS FRAGILE.

The watchmaker, a small, spare man, whose white
hair and unlined face suggested old age and at the same
time no age at all, finished his business with Mr.
Mortimer—which involved a number of wrist and pocket
watches which the antiquarian took from his pockets—and
came over to us. "What can I do for you, lady and
gentlemen?" he asked politely.

Before any one of us could answer, Mr. Mortimer
hurried to our side. "They are with me," he said quickly,
"and have nothing to sell."

"I see," said the watchmaker. "Nevertheless," he
added courteously turning to Herbie, "may I see your
watch, good gentleman?"

Herbie shrugged and, slipping his wristwatch from

his wrist, handed it over. The old man examined it
carefully, held it to his ear, shook it, and held it to his
ear again. "A good watch," he said finally. "But it is
losing time."

I looked around the room at the many clocks all
showing a different hour. "All your clocks are losing
time," I said. "Or else, gaining it, I don't know which."

The watchmaker followed my glance and smiled.
"Ah," he said, "so it must appear to you. But you see,
my friend—if I may call you that—time is not the same
everywhere. For instance—what time is it now in
Timbuctoo? Or on Aldebaran?"

"Aldebaran?" murmured Cordelia uncertainly.

"You yourself," continued the watchmaker, "noticed
how, in my little merry-go-round, the figures did not
always move at the same speed. Yet the clock itself was
all of a piece, the works dependent on the same set of
weights and balances. Would you believe, there was a
time when the lion was fastest of all? The eagle, too, has
slowed down; only the elephant lumbers along, neither
faster nor slower than before.

"No, my friend, time is not the same for everyone.

"You see," he concluded, "it is not really a passage
of little clicks and chimes, which we call hours, or light
and dark, which we call days. Rather, it is a great open
space like the sea, or like the heavens themselves, in

which move all manner of currents, from the majestic tides to sudden whirlpools, some swift, some slow, appearing and disappearing in all directions. What time is it on Cassiopeia? How many seasons has a rose? How many years has a mite? There is no firm answer: everything is relative."

Cordelia turned to me. "I remember once," she said, "your trying to tell me something about time, and I didn't understand it."

"And do you now?" I asked.

"Some of it, I think," she said. "That bit about how many seasons has a rose . . . It all depends on the rose, doesn't it? Like my Countess Vandal at home . . . Where it is, the climate, and the soil . . . I've seen a Sarabande bloom all through a winter in Dorset. It was set against a wall, in the sun. But Cassiopeia . . . ?"

The watchmaker was studying Herbie's watch; he had pried the back cover off and was examining the inner works through a jeweler's eyeglass. He held the watch in one hand, and in the other a slender tool, a delicate screwdriver, with which he tapped the case from time to time. "The mainspring," he said, "is all but worn out. It is likely to go at any moment; I only wonder that it has lasted as long as it has. I believe that it has been doctored. . . ."

"I am sick to death of doctors," said Herbie abruptly.

"I never found one who seemed to know the cause of
my various distresses or what to do about them."

He gestured wearily. "By now," he said, "I have one
of the most extensive collections of pills in the country.
They come in all sizes, colors, and shapes; I have one
especially compounded for me by a native Brazilian doctor
in the jungles of the Amazon."

"If I were to touch the spring ever so lightly," said
the watchmaker, "it would break."

His hand with the tiny screwdriver was poised above
the watch. I gazed at him in consternation; his face,
bland, ageless, was without expression, but it seemed to
me that his eyes shone for a moment with an icy light.
Cordelia at my side gave a gasp of dismay; Herbie alone
appeared indifferent. Mr. Mortimer was not: he moved at
once to seize the watchmaker's hand.

"Give it back," he said.

The watchmaker pursed his lips, and drew back the
hand which held the watch. "No," he said. And he added
quietly, "The spring is almost gone."

"There is still time," said Mr. Mortimer obstinately.
"Give it back to the gentleman."

"And if I don't?" asked the watchmaker.

"Then you are interfering with my business," said
Mr. Mortimer, "and it is not your business to interfere."

The watchmaker held Herbie's watch by its band

and swung it idly to and fro. "Just the same," he declared, "I am better at telling time than you are. The watch is already done with."

"There is still a tick in it," said Mr. Mortimer. "Listen."

And it seemed to me that in all that hum and chiming I could indeed hear Herbie's watch ticking: one . . . two . . . three . . . very faintly.

"Ah, but so slowly," said the watchmaker. "So slowly."

He turned his icy stare on Mr. Mortimer. "Besides," he said, "what is it to you? Since I shall have it anyway . . ."

I felt Cordelia tug at my arm. "Look at Herbie," she breathed.

He was staring at his watch as though hypnotized. "Don't," he whispered. "Don't put more needles in me."

He rose slowly to his feet. "I've got to reach Ruth," he said and, turning, suddenly made for the door.

Mr. Mortimer snatched the watch from the watchmaker's hand and, with an exclamation, "Now you've done it!", rushed after Herbie with Cordelia and myself hard on his heels. So hard, in fact, that we collided in the doorway and by the time we'd sorted ourselves out, Herbie had disappeared.

It was very cold in the street, with a black wind

sweeping along the pavement. "Look," I said to Mr. Mortimer, "there's no use our staying all three of us together. Will you take my wife home? I'll go after Herbie myself and bring him back to the house."

"Gladly," said the antiquarian, "for I can see that the lady is shivering with cold."

I kissed Cordelia's cold cheek, and she clung to me for a moment. "Your nose is wet," she said. "It's lovely."

I helped her into Mr. Mortimer's van, and they started back the way we had come. "Take care," she said.

I turned in the other direction, and at that moment a police patrol car appeared at the end of the street and rolled slowly toward me. I stood and waited for it; when it reached me, it stopped and I realized that I was being carefully examined by the burly but shadowy constable behind the wheel. Since I couldn't see him very well in the dimly lit interior, the advantage was all on his side. "Do you have business hereabouts, mister?" he asked suspiciously.

I told him that I was searching for a friend. "Male or female?" he asked. His voice was, on the whole, unfriendly, and I felt a little stiffening in my spine. "Does it matter?" I asked.

"It might," he said, "in a manner of speaking. Because of the lateness of the hour. And whether your friend is expecting you. And so forth. Section 7,

Paragraph 143: 'One law shall be to him that is homeborn, and to the stranger that sojourns.' "

"As a matter of fact," I said resentfully, "my friend is an old man as well as a stranger, and I have to find him."

"Walk before me," said the constable.

"Why?" I demanded.

"Because," he said, "walking is not allowed hereabouts."

"Not allowed?" I protested. "Why not?"

"I don't answer questions," said the constable coldly. "I'm the Law.

"What's more," he added, "I don't make the rules. I just pass them on to you and see that you observe them. And help you to get from here to there."

"You say you're the Law," I said obstinately. "Let's see your shield."

"I am your shield," he said. "And I am what I am. And I tell you not to walk abroad at night; not in this city, nor in any city in this land. It's too dangerous; there are too many nuts around, laying in wait. Drug users, malicious mischief makers. Just the other day, a householder in this town had the windshield of his Cadillac busted in bright daylight by a Jebusite."

"A Jebusite?" I asked incredulously.

"Could be," said the constable. "Or maybe an

Egyptian or a Moabite. There's a lot of malice in the
world. I didn't put it there, but I know how to use it.
An eye for an eye and a tooth for a tooth. You'd better
stick to me; I'll get you where you're going. Just obey the
Law, that's all."

He put his car in gear. "You stand over there," he
said, "by that rock, and I'll go by, and when you see my
tail lights, you follow them. Just don't stray, that's all."

Chapter 12

HE moved slowly ahead of me down the street and out of the town, and I followed his tail lights. *And the Lord went before them to lead them the way; and by night in a pillar of fire . . .* The road, if there was a road, seemed to climb gently in the empty desert-darkness. After a while, he stopped and pointed toward a darker shadow off to one side. "There's your friend," he said. "Up on yonder slope."

The night was just beginning to turn gray; day was already risen over Kansas, a thousand miles away. "So long," he said.

"Be good."

And with a wave of his arm, he turned back to town again.

I found Herbie huddled on the ground, with his back
to a tree. "Old friend," he said, "we have come into the
shadowy part of the woods."

"I know, Admiral," I said.

He smiled ever so slightly. "The path could end
suddenly," he said.

We sat staring down at a formless land still in its
pool of light. The cold of the last hour before dawn
was all around us, and our breath made little puffs of fog
in the gray air. Herbie sighed. "What was it all about,
Bobby?" he asked. "I swear, I don't know."

"I don't either, Admiral."

"I'm afraid," he said after a while. "And I don't
know what of. Perhaps I only thought that I was going
somewhere, that I had something to do . . . that there
was a reason, that I was going to find something. If only
Ruth had told me. Perhaps I didn't listen. . . . Somehow, in
these years, we've told each other less, or else I've
listened less. . . . And my life—in and out of bureaus
and offices, in and out of libraries, with the taste of anger
in my mouth . . . always. Or home again, to a choke of
dryness. Is that all I have to remember?"

"No," I said.

He didn't seem to hear me. "What good was it?" he
said. "I've watched the dissolution of the world between
two wars. I've watched the disintegration of my country.

ROBERT NATHAN

I've seen the face of art turn to a hideous grimace, the
sound of music into devilish shrieks. I've seen corruption
in high places, the arrogance of the young, the surrender
of the old; I've watched the abandonment of manners,
the contempt for habit and custom. I've felt the terror of
a world without God, the despair of a world without
justice; I've seen the rise of naked power, the emergence
of lunatics who would liefer kill than not. I have lived
to see blackmailers acquitted, pirates unhanged, murderers
befriended, and traitors acclaimed. I have seen whites
cowering before blacks; I have seen the end of the world
poised upon a handful of launching pads."

He was silent a moment, staring bleakly before him.
The air about us grew lighter; in the east there was the
faintest suggestion of color in the sky. A small, cold wind
blew in on us, ahead of the dawn. "The end of innocence,"
he said. "I have seen the end of innocence. What am I
waiting for?

"*Boruch Adonai*," he whispered. And turning to me,
"I wish I could believe," he said wistfully. "The wise, the
loving Father, the Lord of Hosts, with a Jewish son . . .
what a comfort!"

He smiled faintly. "Only a few hundred years ago,"
he said, "it would have been so easy. Since the world
itself was thought to be only five thousand years old.

Eli, Eli, Adonai Elohenu. All because of a book no older
than Homer's Iliad. But the world is older than five
thousand years; and the universe is measureless."

His head drooped forward and he appeared to doze
for a moment. He seemed utterly spent. "And yet," he
said, rousing himself, "I can't believe that He is
indifferent. After all, you found me here. Was it only
by chance?"

"A constable brought me," I said.

He nodded thoughtfully. "A constable," he said. "Of
course. One who draws his authority from a higher
source. Do you realize how many bureaus one has to go
through? I know, because I was near the top myself.
F.D.R. called me Herbert.

"And even then—in the end—where *is* the top? One
wants so much to believe . . . not in something bleaker
and emptier than the holes between the stars, but in
something with the taste and feel of earth . . . to know
that it is there . . . somewhere. That it is there."

He was silent again, remembering. "You know," he
said at last, "I used to rescue bees from my pool in York.
It was a big pool and they fell in and I pulled them out.
Not always; sometimes I forgot or I didn't see them. . . .
They must have thought—if they thought at all—that
some incomprehensible and indifferent power saved some

and let others drown. I couldn't talk bee-talk and so I couldn't tell them. And I suppose it was true that in a sense I was indifferent. Yet I felt pity and sorrow for those I let drown. . . .

"It's a poor analogy, of course. But I like to think that at the end, before they fell asleep in the water, they remembered some particular morning in summer, when the sun was especially warm and the scent of flowers unusually sweet. . . ."

He broke off and raised his head inquisitively; he seemed to be sniffing at the air. "That's odd," he said.

"What is it, Herbie?"

"A memory . . . the smell of something . . ."

The hollow of mist below us had cleared; the sky was yellow in the east, blue overhead; morning was on us, the air was clear and fresh. And down below us, just touched by the morning light, was an old wooden verandahed house with a thin curl of smoke rising from the chimney. I heard Herbie give a little cry deep in his throat. "It's our house, Bobby," he said. "Our first house. The one in Kansas. And Ruth is cooking a ham. I can smell it.

"Come along, old fellow; she's waiting for us!"

I took a few steps with him, and then let him go on by himself. Halfway there, Mr. Mortimer's van caught up with him, and he stepped into it, and they went on

together toward the house. They hadn't reached it when
I turned back.

"You were gone for a long time," said Cordelia.
"Did you have a good walk?"

I stared at her in confusion. The sun was shining
into the breakfast room, and the sea and the sky were
very blue outside our windows. She looked as she always
did in the morning, flower-fresh and a little pink from
sleep. "Yes," I said. "I suppose I did."

She had been cooking a breakfast of ham and eggs,
and the good smell filled the room. "There was a
message," she said, "while you were out. A telegram,
from Larry. They phoned it in."

"Herbie?" I asked, and she nodded. "Yes," I said.
"I know."

"I told them to mail it to us," she declared. "It said
he died early this morning. I wired Ruth at York and sent
our love. That was right, wasn't it, darling?"

"Yes," I said.

"Shall we go east to the funeral, do you think?"

"No," I said. "I don't think so."

"You were such old friends," she said. "All of you:
Ruth, Larry, Herbie, yourself . . . I'm glad he had no
pain at the end. I mean . . . it would have been peaceful,
wouldn't it? Not knowing where he was?"

"It was peaceful," I said.

"What time is it now in the east?" she asked. "There's three hours' difference . . . isn't there? So, if it were early in the morning there, it would still be dark out here . . .? Or is it the other way 'round? I never know. . . . And what time is it on Cassiopeia?"

She lifted her head in the way she had and stared me straight in the eye, and I stared back at her. Cassiopeia? *The watchmaker . . .!*

So she had been there after all; it had all been real. And yet I knew by that lifted, challenging look, that we would never talk about it. It would have opened too many doors . . . opening onto—what? There were no answers.

"I must get after the aphids on my roses," she said.

I believe—and I think she does, too—that what cannot be explored is best left undisturbed.

Two days later we had a letter from Ruth. "The end came very simply," she wrote. "He had been in a coma for two days, and at about nine he seemed to come half awake, or perhaps he didn't, and he said something so strange. He said 'There were pineapples in it.' I've no idea what he meant. But I do think he smiled, ever so slightly. And afterward he looked so peaceful. Larry was with me, and a great comfort, and I asked him to wire you."

And in a tiny scrawl, at the bottom of the page, she had added:

"I wish he'd said he loved me."

But of course, in his way, he had. I must write and tell her so.

Books by Robert Nathan

NOVELS

1973 *The Summer Meadows*
1971 *The Elixir*
1970 *Mia*
1967 *Stonecliff*
1965 *The Mallot Diaries*
1964 *The Fair*
1963 *The Devil with Love*
1962 *A Star in the Wind*
1961 *The Wilderness-Stone*
1960 *The Color of Evening*
1958 *So Love Returns*
1956 *The Rancho of the Little Loves*
1955 *Sir Henry*
1953 *The Train in the Meadow*

1951 *The Innocent Eve*
1950 *The Married Look*
1950 *The Adventures of Tapiola*
      containing *Journey of Tapiola, 1938*
      and *Tapiola's Brave Regiment, 1941*
1949 *The River Journey*
1948 *Long After Summer*
1947 *Mr. Whittle and the Morning Star*
1943 *But Gently Day*
1942 *The Sea-Gull Cry*
1941 *They Went on Together*
1940 *Portrait of Jennie*
1938 *Winter in April*
1938 *The Barly Fields*
      containing *The Fiddler in Barly, 1926*
      The Woodcutter's House, 1927
      The Bishop's Wife, 1928
      The Orchid, 1931
      and *There is Another Heaven, 1929*
1936 *The Enchanted Voyage*
1935 *Road of Ages*
1933 *One More Spring*
1925 *Jonah*

POEMS

1973 *Evening Song*
1950 *The Green Leaf*

1945 *The Darkening Meadows*
1944 *Morning in Iowa*
1941 *Dunkirk*
1940 *A Winter Tide*
1935 *Selected Poems*
1929 *A Cedar Box*
1922 *Youth Grows Old*

THEATER

1966 *Juliet in Mantua*
1953 *Jezebel's Husband & The Sleeping Beauty*

FOR YOUNG PEOPLE

1968 *Tappy*
1959 *The Snowflake and the Starfish*

ARCHAEOLOGY

1960 *The Weans*

74-781

F
N
Nathan, Robert

The summer meadows

DATE			

WITHDRAWN

© THE BAKER & TAYLOR CO.